The HOUSE NEXT TO THE FACTORY

Celebrating
30 Years of Publishing
in India

Praise for The House Next to the Factory

What links Sonal Kohli's beautiful, perspicacious stories is an aspirational India informed by historical and economic change. Sonal is very shrewd when it comes to grasping her characters' desires and failings, and also the subtle ways in which their decisions are either enabled or thwarted by their history and by new opportunities. She has a way of absorbing the reader in her world, and also revealing very delicately how that world is surprising, unexpected, and in flux. I think the strength of many of her stories lies in the way that they are about very little, and about ordinary people, so that the interregnum described seems to capture something that's vital but only partly perceptible from a distance.

– AMIT CHAUDHURI

Sonal Kohli tells all the truth slant and the result is a very fine collection of stories about a set of seemingly commonplace lives whose patterns and rhythms convince the reader that there is an alleviating charm, perhaps even hope for redemption, in the subdued and careful noticing of the ordinary.

– ANJUM HASAN

Here is a fully realized world with many vivid characters observed with sensitivity and grace. And the storytelling is utterly immersive. One of the most pleasurable works of fiction I've read in a long time.

– CHANDRAHAS CHOUDHURY

Thoughtful, delicate and wide-ranging, *The House Next to the Factory* is a paean to quiet lives everywhere and a testament to the often-overlooked power of the ordinary.

– MADHURI VIJAY

Beautifully crafted and written, with so much meaning and so many possibilities imbued in every sentence.

– MANIL SURI

I loved *The House Next to the Factory*. I think it was Maupassant who asked Balzac how he should write and Balzac replied: 'Just take a walk to the market square and minutely observe and describe each detail.' Sonal Kohli captures the grain of lived reality. And there is this simplicity bordering on sublimity.

– NEELUM SARAN GOUR

In quietly ambitious prose, Sonal Kohli charts the turbulent three decades of a 'rising' India. *The House Next to the Factory* is one of the very rare fictions to examine the immense human costs – profound emotional and psychological disorientations – that the Indian bourgeoisie has paid for its material success.

– PANKAJ MISHRA

In prose that is spare yet astutely detailed, Kohli evokes entire lives through just a few deft strokes. Finely hewn, these stories carry a lingering effect.

– SHARANYA MANIVANNAN

[A] collection of stories that is one of the most human and heartening embodiments of what language and narrative can do with the great paradox of the banal ... This is a book that asks whether literature is an immersion into the quotidian or a violation of it, only to show that literature is both, and that there really is no conflict between them ... It is the tantalising balance of stillness and the (never quite realised) lure of drama that makes *The House Next to the Factory* a very special book ... The lightly stirred eddies of life keep moving in the fiction of the writers scattered through these stories: Henry Green, R.K. Narayan, V.S. Pritchett, Amrita Pritam, Anton Chekhov. The swirl of art that comes alive in this constellation says a lot about the aesthetic of Kohli's stories, drawing them into a tender and intimate tradition of world literature.

– SAIKAT MAJUMDAR, *The Hindu*

An ambitious and confident debut ... [B]y borrowing from the best techniques of short- and long-form fiction [Kohli] manages to create something unique that feels organic and true to the lived human existence in all its multihued and sordid splendour ... The stripped-down prose is effective and instrumental in guiding the delighted reader into the inner lives of these characters. A lesser writer would have tried to cram in exposition but Kohli is that rare talent who exercises remarkable restraint to let each story just be, thereby amplifying the magic considerably, pulling off something truly special.

– ANUJA CHANDRAMOULI, *The New Indian Express*

William Boyd once wrote of Chekhov that he refused to judge or explain, depicting life as he saw it in all its banality and tragicomedy. In the same way, as with the character in one story who carefully pieces a jigsaw puzzle together, Kohli's book constitutes a vivid and remarkable picture of people who are often considered unremarkable.

– SANJAY SIPAHIMALANI, *Money Control*

The best writers of short fiction are masters at creating telescopic narratives, and Kohli has honed this craft with care and attention ... *The House Next to the Factory* brings fresh energy into the landscape of Indian writing in English.

– SOMAK GHOSHAL, *Mint Lounge*

[A]n amazing assemblage of discrete yet somewhat interconnected stories ... Kohli's gift as a writer is that she is able to narrate the commonplace everyday lives of her characters by capturing, in and through them, what remains the essentially ungraspable, as she invites the readers to unhurriedly participate in the lives of the characters she so warmly etches in her book.

– *The Book Review*

Most fiction treats time linearly, some restructure it. Kohli compresses time. She makes the distant past, the recent past, and the present indistinguishable. Scenes across periods are woven together so effortlessly that the stories become snapshots where time stands still and the past and the present are seen together ... [A] beautiful example of how much can be achieved through sparing prose.

– *Hindustan Times*

Kohli is not interested in what messes us up but rather what holds us together along one tight, unbroken seam. In this collection of nine short stories, one that successfully manages to capture the emotional mood of a nation from the early '70s to nearly the present day, Kohli wields both brevity and ambition to present a simple argument: life is what happens to us when we are most attentive and in sync with the changes threatening the scales on which the living world is balanced ... In *The House Next to the Factory*, you will encounter worlds that might be precisely yours, if only you are brave enough to acknowledge their simplicity. Kohli's characters will equally echo in the clang of your kitchen's old brassware on a weekend, the dusty mirror faithfully capturing your family in flux.

– *India Today*

In her first collection of fiction, *The House Next to the Factory*, Sonal Kohli brings us very close to her characters. They are so close, we can feel them breathing ... In its detail, Kohli's prose is sometimes reminiscent of Amit Chaudhuri. Like Chaudhuri, she takes us into the living rooms I grew up in in India. But as easily, she wears the uncertain adulthood of an Indian in the twenty-first century. What is present is a constant referencing between individuals to their inanimate surroundings and to other humans, people searching for one another or taking another's presence for granted, bewildered by the connection but like magnets unable to stay apart. This flickering heat is subtle, but coupled with the sweet detail of her prose, Kohli entices.

– *World Literature Today*

The HOUSE NEXT TO THE FACTORY

SONAL KOHLI

FOURTH ESTATE • *New Delhi*

First published in hardback in India by Fourth Estate 2021
An imprint of HarperCollins *Publishers*
4th Floor, Tower A, Building No. 10, DLF Cyber City,
DLF Phase II, Gurugram, Haryana – 122002
www.harpercollins.co.in

This edition published in India by Fourth Estate 2023

2 4 6 8 10 9 7 5 3 1

Some of the stories in this book have been previously published in slightly different form: 'Morning Visitor' in *The Caravan*, 'One Hour, Three Times a Week' in *Unthology 7*, '10 Bela Road' in *Blackbird*, 'The Outing' in *Bristol Short Story Prize Anthology Volume 12*, and an excerpt from 'Kettle on the Hob' as 'Living in the Countryside' in *Monkeybicycle*.

P-ISBN: 978-93-5699-413-3
E-ISBN: 978-93-5422-852-0

Typeset in 10.5/15.6 Scala (OTF) at
Manipal Technologies Limited, Manipal

Printed and bound at
Thomson Press (India) Ltd

For my parents,

Radhey Sham and Sunita Aggarwal

With her inner eye she saw how her own house and its particular history linked and contained her as well as her whole family with all their separate histories and experiences – not binding them within some dead and airless cell but giving them the soil in which to send down their roots, and food to make them grow and spread, reach out to new experiences and new lives, but always drawing from the same soil, the same secret darkness.

– Anita Desai, *Clear Light of Day*

ONE HOUR, THREE TIMES A WEEK

THE HOUSE HAD TWO gates. There was a large rust-coloured one, past which Mr Lamba could see nothing. It seemed like the entrance to the factory. A few metres ahead was a small white gate with a square grille at the top. Mr Lamba walked his scooter to the smaller gate and parked it. He peeked in through the grille. There was an oval, grassless lawn and an empty veranda. He tried the doorbell, but the switch was stuck. Mr Lamba lifted the latch and went inside.

He knocked at the glass door. In the kitchen, to his left, a yellow fridge hummed loudly. There were two Campa Cola bottle magnets on the fridge.

A boy of eight or nine came to the door.

'Is your father at home?' Mr Lamba said.

'He's at the factory. You should use the other gate.' The boy was barefoot.

'Is your mother at home?'

'Yes, wait.' He ran inside, leaving Mr Lamba standing there holding his helmet.

The grassless lawn was lined with rose shrubs on one side. Two children's cycles leaned against the veranda wall.

'Yes?' The mother appeared at the door. She had a round face, just like her son. She wore a blue sari with big, pink flowers on it.

'I'm Naresh Lamba.' He cleared his throat. 'I'm a schoolteacher, and I provide private tuitions as well. Your husband, I think, left his card for me at Satnam Stationers.'

'Ah, yes. He spoke about it. Come in, please.'

The living area was long and narrow, like a passage, with a dining table on the near side and black Rexine sofas on the far one. He and the mother settled down on the sofas. There was a money plant in the corner with large, waxy leaves.

'My sister-in-law and I are looking for a tutor for our sons,' the mother said. 'They are the same age.'

'Would you like me to tutor them together or separately?'

'You can teach them together and charge for one-and-a-half pupils. That's how their last tutor worked.'

'Which class are they in?'

'They just started third grade. How long have you been teaching, sir?'

'It's been twenty-five years. My subjects are maths and English, but I can help with others as well.'

'Okay. But they are a bit naughty, so you'll have to be strict.'

'Don't worry about that.' Mr Lamba laughed and adjusted his glasses.

She called out to the boys.

Three doors on the long wall opposite led into the bedrooms. Mr Lamba folded his arms over his stomach and waited for the boys to emerge. On the showcase a glass heron bent and rose periodically as it sipped from a trough. It was a lulling movement.

An old woman came out of the middle room and sat down on the sofa.

'Namaste,' Mr Lamba said.

The woman nodded but said nothing. There was a slit in the side of her nose where she must have once worn a heavy nose ring.

'Raghu and Anuj's new tutor,' the young woman said to the older one.

The boys came and stood by the mother. 'This is Raghu,' she said, pointing to the boy with full cheeks. He was still barefoot. 'And this is my sister-in-law's son, Anuj.' Anuj had a thin, dusky face and a staple-sized scar on his chin. The cousins smiled at Mr Lamba. Both were missing some teeth.

'So we start next Monday, boys?' Mr Lamba said.

The boys nodded.

MR LAMBA GOT OUT of bed and stretched his arms. At home it was his habit to wear just a vest and pajama, and when winter came he wrapped a shawl over the vest. He arched his back, straightened, and twisted to the right then to the left. His son was still sleeping on the other divan. Mr Lamba folded the top sheet and patted the pillow.

He made two cups of tea and took one to his mother. He helped her sit up.

'Everything okay, Roop Kumar?' She addressed Mr Lamba as her brother who was lost during Partition, the only person she seemed to remember these days.

'Yes, everything okay.'

He took his cup outside and sat in a chair and drank the tea. He contemplated the two sparrows that pecked at each other on the boundary wall. It was warm for April. The sun shone brightly. For the last week, he had been reminding himself to water the tulsi that sat next to the gate. The leaves were turning brown at the edges.

The morning paper, rolled and secured with an elastic band, landed with a thud in the little veranda.

Mr Lamba read the headlines as he finished his tea. Sikh militants had attacked a bus of Hindu pilgrims in Punjab, shooting the conductor and two male passengers. Mr Lamba skimmed through the details.

He put the cups in the sink and helped his mother to the bathroom. Her skin had become loose and hung from her bones in thin pleats. A maid came twice a week to give her a bath.

He dusted the dining table and chairs, the switchboard, and the centre table between the two divans. With gentle strokes, he brushed the crochet wall hanging his wife had made one winter. He wiped the cupboards in his mother's room and the side tables crammed against the walls. There were only two bedrooms in the house. After his wife passed away two years ago, he had given his room to his daughter. He finished cleaning the windowpanes and joined her in the kitchen. He kneaded the dough and rolled the chapatis, while she prepared a sabzi of potatoes and beans. His son was in the bathroom, splashing himself with mugs full of water. He was an accountant in a small firm. Mr Lamba shared his shirts with him. They were snug for Mr Lamba but loose for his son, who at twenty-three was still lanky. The only household errand the son did was to sew buttons on the shirts whenever they went missing.

Mr Lamba packed his lunch, got ready, and left for work.

MR LAMBA ARRIVED AT five sharp for the first tutorial. He parked his scooter outside the smaller gate. The road was dusty and busy with traffic, and factory workers walked home carrying tin lunchboxes. Down the street was Campa Cola's Delhi plant – white façade, a trim of red.

Mr Lamba tried the doorbell, then lifted the latch and went inside.

In the kitchen, the cook was chopping vegetables. He wore grey overalls, like a factory hand.

Mr Lamba knocked briefly at the glass door and entered. He found Raghu and Anuj jumping from one sofa to the next, like a pair of kangaroos, and a little girl of about four running around the coffee table. Mr Lamba cleared his throat.

'Good evening, sir.' The boys climbed down. The girl hid behind them and peeked from the side. 'My sister, Kavya,' Raghu said.

'Good evening, all of you. Bring your books, boys.' Mr Lamba sat down on the long sofa. 'And you put on your slippers,' he said to Raghu. He had left dusty paw prints on the black seats.

Mr Lamba placed his helmet and cloth bag under the coffee table. Faint notes of an English song emanated from the room near the sofas.

The boys brought their schoolbags and settled on either side of him. Raghu was wearing his mother's flip-flops, which were two sizes too big for him.

'We'll start with English.' He asked them to read a paragraph each from the text.

Both the boys read haltingly, and Anuj had trouble stringing the letters together. Mr Lamba realized he would have to work hard with them. He explained the text and dictated answers to the questions at the back, while the boys took notes kneeling by the coffee table. The songs continued to play lightly.

The cook brought a cup of tea.

'Can you please bring some biscuits?' Mr Lamba said to him. 'I get gas if I don't eat with my evening tea.'

'I'll get some for you, sir,' Anuj said, jumping up.

'You study.' He pressed Anuj down by the shoulder and smiled at the cook.

The music stopped and a dusky woman emerged from the room. She had fine collarbones. 'They are always trying to run away from their books,' she said. 'Namaste, sir. I'm Anuj's mother.' She looked at the books spread on the table. 'His grammar and spellings need special attention.'

'Don't worry.' Mr Lamba picked the skin off the tea. 'He has good handwriting though.'

Anuj stuck out his tongue at his mother.

'That's true.' She smiled and returned to her room. This time she shut the door.

Mr Lamba dunked the biscuits and sipped the tea. The boys memorized the answers they had noted down, sitting with their feet up on the sofa. On the right-hand wall was a set of double doors with a brass bolt across the middle. 'Is this a cupboard?' Mr Lamba said. He had missed it on the first visit.

The cousins laughed. Raghu slid off the sofa and unbolted the doors.

Mr Lamba shifted his weight to see. A set of stairs led up and disappeared into darkness. An old pressure cooker sat on the first step. On the other side were pairs of worn shoes. A badminton racket lay on the step above, and above that a torn cushion with the sponge showing.

'The stairs go up to the terrace,' Raghu said.

'The terrace door is burnt like Mrs Venkatraman's arm, sir,' Anuj said.

'Who is Mrs Venkatraman?'

'She teaches maths at school,' Raghu said.

Mr Lamba imagined the blistered skin of Mrs Venkatraman's arm.

'Our cook was smoking a beedi and he threw it and the newspaper pile at the top of the stairs caught fire,' Anuj told Mr Lamba.

'We sometimes take our bicycles to the terrace, sir,' Raghu said. 'The terrace is small, but if we go round in circles, like on the lawn, we can cycle for a long time without stopping.'

'Is there no park close by where you can go?'

Raghu shook his head. He shut the door and came and sat in his place. 'We are not allowed to go out of the house alone, sir, not even to look for our cricket balls.'

Mr Lamba nodded. It was an industrial area. There were factories up and down the road and no houses in the vicinity. Workers lingered at tea stalls and Mr Lamba had seen some of them smoking outside factory gates. It wouldn't be safe for the boys to be out by themselves, but he could understand how suffocating it must be for them to be cooped up at home. He looked from Anuj to Raghu. They were trying to memorize the answers, eyes clenched, rocking back and forth. He wished he could take them out one afternoon but knew that it would be inappropriate.

The grandmother came and sat at the dining table. Mr Lamba put aside the cup and resumed the lesson.

A WEEK LATER, ON his way back from the tuition, Mr Lamba stopped at Satnam Stationers. With the helmet under his arm, he waited while Satnam Singh packed red and green glaze papers, gum and golden sprinkle for a girl who stood on this side of the counter. Satnam slipped a pink flier into the bag before handing it to the girl.

'How are you?' Mr Lamba said, as the girl skipped away.

'Same as ever.' Satnam lifted the counter flap and Mr Lamba walked in. He sat down on the extra stool. Above a jar of pencils hung the pink flier he had taped there a month ago, asking parents and students to contact him for home tuitions. Below the note was the sketch of a man on a scooter. Mr Lamba looked bulky even in the sketch.

'I got the tuition job,' he said.

'Very good, very good, sir.' Satnam looked up from the ledger, tucking his ballpoint pen between his ear and black turban. 'We must celebrate.' He sent the shop help to get tea and samosas.

'I'm tutoring two little boys ... Thank you, Satnam.' He took the stationer's hand and patted it. It was Satnam's idea that Mr Lamba start home tuitions. After his wife's death, he found it difficult to pass the time at home. He would correct the school notebooks, put a chair outside and watch the street, come in and lie on the divan, but the long evenings refused to end. Satnam even allowed him to include his phone number on the flier as Mr Lamba did not have a phone at home.

They ate the samosas. A hot breeze was blowing, making the trees rustle. The two talked about the weather and the long power cuts and about Rakesh Sharma's satellite call to Mrs Gandhi from outer space. Like always, they kept away from the subject of politics, the militancy in Punjab and the Sikhs' demand for a separate nation. Satnam brushed the samosa crumbs off the counter.

Mr Lamba finished the tea, bought a packet of red ballpoint pens and left for home.

RAGHU AND ANUJ LAY on the sofa, watching cricket. Their grandmother and Anuj's mother were at the dining table, playing cards, possibly rummy. The mother had a white bandage around her palm. Mr Lamba wanted to ask what happened, but he only cleared his throat.

'Namaste, sir,' she said. The grandmother glanced at the clock. The boys sprang from the sofa, turned off the TV, and scrambled to the rooms for their books.

Mr Lamba said namaste to the mother and grandmother and went to sit at the sofa.

The boys settled on either side of him. 'Good evening, sir,' they said.

'Take out your maths books. We'll do unitary method sums today.'

He told Raghu to read out the first problem.

'If ten chocolates cost twenty rupees, how much would three chocolates cost?'

'So, Anuj.' Mr Lamba put his arm around the boy. 'What do you think? Would it cost less than twenty or more?'

Anuj stroked his chin. 'Less?'

'Yes. Good. Now to solve this problem, we need to first find the price of one chocolate.'

He wrote down:

10 chocolates cost Rs. 20

∴ 1 chocolate costs 20 ÷ 10

'In the unitary method, we first find the price of one unit. Now to calculate the price of three chocolates, we multiply the above by three. And there's your answer: six rupees.'

The boys nodded.

He told Anuj to read out the next problem.

The boys watched as Mr Lamba's red pen worked fluently on the page, dividing and multiplying. They worked out five sums together.

'Did you get that?' He looked at the boys over his glasses. He wrote them questions to practise. The boys did the calculations kneeling by the coffee table. Mr Lamba sharpened four pencils and set them on the table in a neat row. Raghu's sister appeared, and he offered her a pencil and a loose sheet. She smiled, grabbed the stationery and returned to her mother's room. Mr Lamba folded his arms over his stomach and waited for tea. The glass heron bent and rose.

'I'll be back. Continue with your calculations.' He went to the toilet.

When he returned, Raghu was wearing his helmet and riding the arm of the sofa, with Anuj trying to snatch the helmet off his head.

'What's this?' Mr Lamba said.

Raghu took off the helmet and the boys slipped back into their seats.

Mr Lamba sat down between them and put the helmet under the coffee table. The helmet was scratched, and its white inner shell showed in one place. He cuffed the back of the boys' heads.

'Our last tutor, Mr Bhaskar, used to wear a thick bracelet, sir,' Raghu said without looking up from his notebook. 'Every time he slapped us, his bracelet hit our jaw hard. It hurt more than the slap, sir.'

'Okay, do your sums.' Mr Lamba's stomach growled. The cousins snickered. He wondered if the cook would bring him tea today, but based on the past month, he knew that neither the cook nor the tea could be counted on.

'You know, sir, a monkey bit my mother's hand,' Anuj said.

'How did that happen?' Mr Lamba pushed back his glasses.

'She had just washed her face at the sink in the veranda,' he said, sitting cross-legged on the floor, 'and she reached for the towel on the rail, when this fat monkey sitting on the wall bit her.'

Mr Lamba tsk-tsked.

'She had to get injections,' Raghu said and laughed. Anuj laughed too.

'Okay, enough. Now let me see your notebooks.'

'Two more minutes, sir!' they cried, and stooped over their calculations. Kavya returned with her sheet scribbled with the English alphabet and showed it to Mr Lamba. Mr Lamba put a tick mark in the bottom corner with the red pen, like he would for the boys, and wrote 'V. Good'.

As he was leaving that evening, the grandmother came out of her room. 'There are still five minutes left,' she said.

Mr Lamba glanced at the clock. Its golden hands were shaped like arrows. 'Ah, yes.' But he wasn't sure if he should go back and tell the boys to reopen their books. 'I'll make up for it next time,' he said, and left clutching the helmet under his arm and craving his evening tea.

MR LAMBA SAT OUTSIDE his house in a vest and pajama. The newspaper rested on his knee. The sky was the colour of mud and it looked like there would be a dust storm. The monsoon didn't seem far off. Children were playing hopscotch, the grid drawn with chalk that they must have stolen from school. Their shorts and frocks flapped in the breeze.

His daughter returned from the stenography class. She was having an affair with a man from the neighbourhood. Mr Lamba sometimes saw him drop her home. He had short, greasy hair, and looked like a wrestler with his thick shoulders and the way he held the handlebars of the bike. Mr Lamba didn't have enough money to get a dowry together, so he stayed quiet and let the affair continue. She was wearing maroon lipstick and hoop earrings. Mr Lamba turned his attention to the sports page.

Dust and grit started to blow down the lane. The children laughed and shrieked and ran indoors. Mr Lamba too picked up his chair and went in.

In the kitchen he and his daughter stood side by side, while she made dal and he rolled chapatis, without exchanging a word.

MR LAMBA ARRIVED FOR the lesson at three that afternoon. It was Raghu's birthday and his friends were coming over in the evening to celebrate. When he passed the kitchen, he saw the mother and the cook busy with preparations and the countertop cluttered with dishes and pans.

The living room walls were decorated with strips of crepe paper. A bunch of balloons hung from the fan over the dining table. The three children played with a blue balloon, tossing it in the air and waiting for it to descend.

'Happy birthday,' he wished Raghu. He removed from the cloth bag a box of crayons and an abridged and illustrated copy of *The Adventures of Tom Sawyer*. 'For you.'

'Thank you, sir!'

The cousins sat side by side on the sofa and flipped through the illustrations. Kavya scuttled off with the balloon.

Mr Lamba made them do maps that day, to keep it light because of the boy's birthday. 'On the top, write "Republic of India" in block letters.'

'Do you remember my birthday, sir?' Anuj said.

'It's not for another two months. Do your work.' He had already decided to bring him *Robinson Crusoe*. Satnam had a copy in the shop. Mr Lamba didn't read much himself, not beyond the texts he taught at school, but 'The Last Leaf' was his favourite story. Every year when he read it out to the eighth grade, his heart trembled like the painted leaf on the tree.

The cook brought tea, and a cutlet and jalebi in a side plate.

Mr Lamba sipped the tea and asked the boys about places they knew in India. He showed them how to mark Delhi, in the heart of the country, exactly two finger-widths from the border of Nepal, the nearby state of Punjab, where Raghu's maternal grandparents lived, Himachal, where the hill stations were located, Jammu and Kashmir, where Anuj's father had promised to take him next summer break, Maharashtra, where a cousin lived, and then pointed out the remaining states. While the boys coloured in the states with the new crayons, he sat back and bit into the treats. The jalebi was thick and syrupy. He licked his fingers when he was done.

The hour came to an end and he got up to leave.

'Sir,' Raghu said, as he folded the map and tucked it away in a notebook. 'Come to the terrace. I want to show you how high we got our kite. We've tied it to the water tank.'

Mr Lamba laughed. 'Okay. Go wear your slippers first.'

Anuj slid the bolt and Mr Lamba followed the boys up the stairs. More than the kite, he wanted to see the burnt door. The stairwell smelled dusty. There was no light bulb, and books and newspapers lay in corners, making the stairs narrower. Mr Lamba sidestepped a deflated football. Finally, the boys pushed open the door at the top and ran on to the terrace. The door was charred, sooty. Mr Lamba ran his palm over its uneven surface. The wood had cracked and peeled in many places. Splinters pricked his skin. He felt sorry for the door and for Mrs Venkatraman. He briefly inhaled its burnt odour before following his students to the terrace.

The kite was nowhere in the sky. A coil of thread lay near the water tank. Raghu and Anuj were wrestling each other. Mr Lamba went to stand by the parapet. Beyond the factories were clumps of green groves.

EVERY EVENING BEFORE DINNER, Mr Lamba took two pegs of whisky, a cheap brew that he bought from the government-run store. It was his habit to eat a cucumber as he drank.

When his wife was alive, she would slice the cucumber for him. Now he cut it thickly, without taking off the skin. He sat on the divan drinking and eating the salad. It was raining. Drops slid down the windowpanes. Mr Lamba watched the lizards play on the wall.

THE TOILET WAS TO one side of the house, in a narrow alley that connected the veranda to the factory. The boys' fathers used the passage to come and go. Mr Lamba could see the watchman sitting by the rust-coloured gate and workers unloading sheets of steel from a truck. The boys' fathers made stainless steel utensils. The family had a steel tea set with a golden knob on the pot and a small decanter for milk. Mr Lamba had seen the cook carry tea in it for guests.

He used the toilet, washed his hands and went back into the house.

'Five multiplied by six is thirty, not thirty-five,' he said, glancing at Raghu's notebook. He wiped his hands with his maroon handkerchief.

'Sir,' the grandmother said from the dining table where she sat doing embroidery, 'if you need to urinate, please go outside the gate.'

Mr Lamba looked up.

'Sometimes you don't flush,' she said.

Mr Lamba felt himself going red. The boys continued with their sums, but he could feel their attention on him.

Last week she had said, 'Sir, don't sit on the same sofa every time. The centre seat has started to sag.'

Mr Lamba now sat on a different sofa every week.

She picked up the thread box and embroidery and went to her room.

'Sir.' Raghu pointed to the middle room, then touched his temple and rotated his finger like a screw.

Anuj laughed.

'Don't talk like that about your grandmother.' Mr Lamba folded the handkerchief into four and put it on his knee to dry. The house was so quiet that he could hear machines whirring in the factory and the distant clatter of utensils. He folded the handkerchief further and tucked it into his pocket.

MR LAMBA WAS IN the staffroom correcting notebooks when Mr Chatterjee came in and said, 'Indira Gandhi has been shot by two of her Sikh guards.' Everyone looked at him. Mr Chatterjee liked attention. 'She's critical. They fired at close range.' The three other teachers gathered around him to learn more. Mr Lamba went and stood at the back of the circle.

After the lunch break, he went to the reception and gave the receptionist Raghu's father's number. The receptionist, Miss Patsy, had three fingers missing from her right hand. She dialled with the left one and passed him the receiver. Mr Lamba cleared his throat. He told Raghu's father he would not be coming in that evening. He did not mention the attack.

MR LAMBA SAT AT home following the live broadcast of the state funeral. It was a warm, slow day in November. The radio was on the centre table, with the antenna at forty-five degrees. The announcer said Mrs Gandhi looked peaceful on her last journey. Mr Lamba imagined her hooked nose sticking out of the garlands that had been put around her neck. His son lay on the opposite divan, catching up on the broadcast in between naps. The ceiling fan spun sluggishly.

Over the next few days Hindu mobs attacked and set fire to Sikh neighbourhoods. Eventually a curfew was called. There was no milk at home. Mr Lamba drank black tea for the first time. He didn't like it. He wondered if his mother could tell the difference. During the day he tied old newspapers in a bundle and put aside empty bottles and cans for the kabadiwala, cleaned the refrigerator, washed his scooter, and hoped that Satnam and his family were safe.

WHEN HE WENT TO Raghu and Anuj's for the tuition next week, he saw the Sikh-owned Campa Cola factory gutted. A portion of the white building was covered in soot, the shutters were up, heavy padlocks hung broken. Pieces of furniture and shards of glass littered the compound. A dog lay near the gate, panting.

'I hope everything was okay here,' he said to Raghu's mother, who was at the dining table feeding Kavya a banana. 'It looks like the mob got Campa Cola.'

Raghu raised his head from his notebook. 'Sir, our veranda was full of burnt flakes. They kept falling from the sky. I caught some bits as they fell.'

'Your name will live, Indira,' Anuj sang, 'as long as the sun and moon live.'

Mr Lamba had heard the slogan on the radio. He cuffed the back of Anuj's head. 'Do your sums.'

'We were fine, sir,' the mother said. 'But one of our Sikh workers from the factory came today with his beard shaven and hair cut, my husband told us. He managed it just in time to escape the mob.'

Mr Lamba imagined Satnam without his turban and beard. After the tuition, he went to the shop. The shutter was down.

For a few days Mr Lamba heard the boys hum the slogan as they studied.

MR LAMBA WAS DRIVING back from the tuition. There was a greasy patch in the middle of the road. It shone and twinkled and looked like the large, elongated shadow of a teapot. He thought if he touched it, the grease would come on to his fingers and he could smell and decipher what it was. In staring at the patch, he forgot to avoid it.

He lost control of the scooter and it swerved and fell on its side. The weight came crashing down on his left leg.

A few men standing at the bus stop rushed to help. He winced when they tried to make him stand. His trousers had torn at the shin and there were some blood marks. The men stopped a passing car, put him in the back, and asked the driver to take him to a clinic.

The doctor tapped Mr Lamba's shin and knee with his knuckles and tried to rotate the ankle. He took X-rays and put the leg in a cast. He applied some ointment where Mr Lamba had grazed his palm.

Mr Lamba was confined to bed, like his mother. His leg looked like a cement column. The midterm exams were close, and he worried about the two boys. He requested his son to call Raghu's father and tell him about the accident. He also wanted him to check on Satnam but thought that might be too much to ask.

Lying on the divan, staring at the fan go round, he wondered about the patch of grease. Was it kerosene that a mob had used to burn the Sikhs and their properties?

THE DOORBELL RANG. MR Lamba wrapped the shawl around him, stood up with the help of the crutch, and limped out to see who it was.

The postman gave him a small brown parcel and made him sign on a paper.

Mr Lamba came back to the divan and opened the parcel. There was a ruled sheet inside folded into four, a Campa Cola bottle magnet, and a pocket-sized cricket bat that Mr Lamba knew was Raghu's favourite possession. He ran his fingers over the smooth wood of the bat. He weighed the magnet in his palm.

He put on his glasses and unfolded the letter. It was in Anuj's handwriting.

> *Get well soon sir. We hope the leg is not hurting too much. We have a new tutor. He has a pointed thumbnail. Sometimes he pinches our ears. We miss you always.*
>
> *Yours obediently,*
> *Anuj and Raghu*

Mr Lamba folded the letter and tucked it under his pillow along with the bat and the magnet.

THE OUTING

YOU GET OFF THE rickshaw at the banyan tree outside the post office. From here you plan to find Sister Celina's house on foot. You've applied Band-Aids to the back of your feet where the ballerinas bite. You wear a cream blouse and checked green skirt, your hair in a small ponytail the size of a shaving brush.

You walk past the tiny watch repair shop, the chow mein stall and its sizzling wok. You sidestep a pile of dung. A puppy nibbles at cabbage leaves under a vegetable cart. Women with powdered necks and fresh lipstick haggle over the prices of brinjals and shiny tomatoes. The sounds of Super Mario Bros. – a ding, the mushroom popping – seep out from the grimy curtain of the videogame parlour. Children surround the Kwality ice cream cart that's lit fluorescent green. In the mornings and afternoons when the school bus rolls through, the market is sleepy, but now it's overcome with a busyness that you find intoxicating. You live in an industrial area not far from here, next to the steel factory your family owns. No ice cream carts pass outside your house, no popcorn, no golgappawalas, only lumbering trucks, weary labourers. You spend your evenings playing table tennis against the veranda wall, or embroidering with grandmother whom you like and dislike in turns, and after the factory closes for the day, you sit on the swing that the watchman's son has slung from the neem tree. When the watchman's son sees you, he withdraws to his shack. The watchman allows him outside the factory precincts to fetch tea, to simply cycle, and who knows, maybe he comes as far as the market. You had to make your outing today sound official in order to wheedle permission out of your father, who can be very strict depending on his mood. A man is peeing against the low boundary wall of the cinema. You avert your eyes and quicken your step. Sister Celina's house lies somewhere beyond the market.

Celina was your senior – when you were in the second grade, she was in the tenth. You remember a cold morning when the bus broke down and the girls marched schoolward, she held your hand on one side and another little girl's on the other. Last summer, Sister Catherine introduced her at the afternoon assembly as the ex-student who had returned to the school as a nun. Standing on the lawns, you were startled to see her in the white habit and veil, the cross in a plain black thread resting on her chest. You felt a twinge of sadness. Sister Celina became your chemistry instructor. She paced as she taught, palms clasped, the rope-like veins on the back of her hands evincing an inner strength. She was not an engaging teacher, but she was not stern, and if a girl forgot to bring her textbook, she lent her her own. The textbook was unmarked, she didn't even note her name on the cover, and it made you think how on Sports Day she would board the bus in the afternoon with her medals strung through satin ribbons of red, yellow, aquamarine still around her neck. You wonder often if she had any inkling back then that she would one day become a nun. After the Christmas break, Mrs Nair once again took charge of the chemistry lessons. Sister Celina was no longer seen in the staffroom, and not even in the teal van that ferried the nuns to and from the convent. It was heard that she had undergone gallbladder surgery and was recuperating. But as two months slipped by, there were whispers she had run away with a priest and got pregnant. It was the usual slander about nuns; everyone discussed it, though few trusted it to be true. On the way to a debate competition, the team learned from Mrs Bakshi that actually Sister Celina had an argument with Sister Catherine and was overnight transferred to Paharganj to work with the city's orphans. Mrs Bakshi is jealous of anyone who has the principal's affections. Her transfer theory remains uncorroborated. These days it is being passed about that Sister Celina joined the order after a heartbreak, and having recovered, has returned to her old life. She works at a pathology lab in Moti Nagar, it is said, and has been seen in short skirts and heels. You find yourself thinking about her when you work in the chemistry lab; while you stand in the doorway that connects the house with the factory, watching the sky grow pale and the labourers trickle out through the rust-coloured gate; as you clean your teeth with a neem twig before bed. You're perplexed by the turns her life has taken. Like everyone, you're curious about her disappearance, but your parents would be proud of how you've kept away from gossip.

You pass Kavya Tailors – seeing your name on the signboard always pleases you. The market peters out. A woman waters the twin plants on her gatepost. Boys squat in the dirt, shooting marbles. The rickshawala who brought you here passes by on the other side of the road, spokes sounding tinnily. You glance back: the factories puffing smoke in the distance, tall dark chimneys against the mango sky, look gloomy.

There's nothing remarkable about the lane to your left, but its trees with the cables nestling in the tops and the yellow and pink apartments that give it an overall salmon hue seem to fit with your memory. You turn down it. In the lane, a pair of girls play badminton, and you think of asking them if the Thomases live somewhere here, but two boys lean against a scooter watching the girls, and you feel shy. You are shy of boys – they make you stutter. You walk on, observing the apartments. The drains give off a salty smell that's not wholly unpleasant. Some mornings when Celina was late for the bus, you saw her dash out of her lane, fast as P.T. Usha, while her father hurried after her with her lunchbox. How ordinary that moment was, how beguiling, you think now, Sister Celina was just a girl late for school. You sigh. You rub the back of your right foot where the ballerina is digging in just above the Band-Aid.

Railway Apartments – four storeys high, an exposed cement staircase that looks like vertebrae – could be Sister Celina's building. You glance to check, and it seems like the right distance from the mouth of the lane. The shuttlecock has landed close to the boys, and the one in a cap offers it to the girls as though it were a rose. Even from where you stand, you can hear the girls giggle. You open the rickety gate of the building and cross its dusty compound. You climb the cement stairs, nervous, palm clammy against the banister. On the upper floor, you pick the furthest of the five doors and ring the bell. You clear your throat, wipe your palms on your skirt. The woman who answers the door smells of caramelized onions, has a spatula in hand. In response to your question, she scolds you for ringing the bell. You flush. You stop by the parapet to compose yourself. The sun has dimmed, the trees appear darker. The shuttlecock thwacks back and forth. You inspect above your heel to find a sore spot. You touch its peeling edges. Downstairs, the rickety gate creaks. You glance over the parapet. You squint. You slip your foot back into the ballerina. Is it her? Is it? It is her. It is odd seeing her in regular clothes, to witness her hair, the strands that have come loose from the plait after a long day. She has grocery bags in both hands and a flabby black purse on one shoulder. She looks ordinary, like anyone one might pass in the street. Once again that twinge of sadness. She heaves a hand high enough to fasten the latch. Coriander peeps from a bag. Her footsteps on the stairs are quiet, reminding you of the thick-soled sandals she wore as a nun. Out of the corner of an eye, you glimpse her pass the landing and climb to the second floor. A door opens upstairs and then shuts. In the building across the lane, a bony woman with a child on her hip calls out to a cobbler passing below. You tighten your little ponytail and turn towards the stairs.

Sister Celina appears at the door in a faded nightgown with white and blue flowers. She looks younger without the veil, face delicate, cheekbones pronounced. She has redone her plait since coming home.

'May I come in, please?'

For a second it seems like she'll send you away. Perhaps she doesn't like visitors. Perhaps she remembers you as the girl who spilled ammonium sulphide in the lab, causing it to stink of rotten eggs for days. Something in her shoulders relents then. She nods.

In the living room, a woman is shelling peas. She looks at you as she slits a pod with her thumbnail and empties it into a bowl on the table. You say hello and sit on the adjacent sofa. You hear Sister Celina open the fridge door in the kitchen. There's a TV trolley across from the sofas, the standby light of the VCR glowing. The day's washing rests on the back of a dining chair. The showcase is crammed with knick-knacks, framed photographs and old trophy cups. On one wall is a cross-stitch portrait of a woman by a pond, twilight shades of blue and purple. You would have expected to see in the house some sign of Sister Celina's recent nunhood, her habit and veil on a hanger, laundered, neatly ironed, yet to be put away, or at least a rosary on a side table, her cross. Instead, there are these placid tokens of domesticity, the two women in their nightgowns, and green dirt gathering under the mother's thumbnail. Sister Celina strikes a match in the kitchen, then another one, and finally the flare of the burner. When she returns, you'll start by introducing yourself. When she was teaching you, you didn't remind her you used to share a bus, for though you were once again in the same physical space, it felt like she existed in a realm separate from yours. Now, at last, you can ask her about the nature of life. You will tell her about your dog, who drowned in the acid tank in the workshop and was discovered only the next morning after the factory reopened; the pained sound the swing on the neem makes under your weight; your friend who after a summer in America returned with an accent and forever altered. You want to know if Sister Celina had any intimation that she would one day become a nun. And what caused her now to give up that path. You won't bring up the rumours, for they will hurt her. Instead, you will ask her if she thinks life in the end leads us to a happy place.

She comes to the living room with a soup bowl on a small plate, a steel spoon on the side. She moves the bag of peas to make room in front of her mother, spreads a napkin over her lap, and gestures at her to eat the soup. Sister Celina's eyes meet yours, and in their quietness and in the way she looks down, you sense there have been other visitors, with each of whom she has been respectful, as kind as possible. You want to hold her gaze to let her know you're not here to pry, but the mother is cracking open the pods now *crick-crick* instead of slitting them. Sister Celina tells her again to start with the soup and threads her way to the kitchen. A wisp of steam rises from the bowl and disappears. The cross-stitched woman gazing at the pink stars, it occurs to you, could be the art and craft project the girls do in the eleventh grade for Miss Betsy's class. You wonder if your parents will hang yours until years later, but they are not sentimental about keepsakes – or about you for that matter. The mother continues to crack open the pods; frail wrists, hard knuckles.

Sister Celina returns with two teacups on a tray and offers them to you. You take the one with croutons on top and leave the other that smells like coffee for her. She sits on the third sofa with her cup. She sips it, lips tight, back straight. You want to tell her the soup is good, tomato is your favourite, but it's hard to start a conversation with the pods cracking and the mother's bowl growing steadily cold.

Sister Celina sighs and sets her cup on the table. She walks to the TV trolley, presses the keys on the VCR, then switches on the TV. The mother's heaved herself off the sofa. She hobbles to a switchboard and turns off the tube light. The room is dark now. The walls shift with colours from the screen. Ah, the mother's eating her soup. Sister Celina sips her coffee, more relaxed now, as though she's finally free to savour it. You too lean back into the cushions. The three of you watch the movie clustered around the table, as though it were something you did every evening. The movie is Indian but the characters speak English, the print grainy from being run over and over again. Miss Stoneham, who seems Sister Celina's mother's age, teaches Shakespeare at school and lives alone in her dilapidated apartment with her cat. Outside, the sun sinks and the moon pulleys up, the girls playing badminton return indoors, the rickshawala pedals home a passenger and his new mattress, the air smells damply of roses from the flower stall. Sister Celina fast forwards some scenes, but the mother doesn't mind and you of course can't say anything. You fold your arms and marvel at the fact that you're here instead of at home, and you are surprised at yourself. *'Itsy Bitsy Teenie Weenie Yellow Polkadot Bikini'* plays on an old gramophone as Miss Stoneham's evenings liven up in the company of an ex-pupil and the pupil's boyfriend. Sister Celina sways her foot lightly. The coffee cup rests on the arm of the sofa, her flip-flop dangles from her toes. She appears at ease in her nightgown, on the sofa, in this TV-lit house that smells of stale bread. The mother places her napkin and empty bowl on the table. You glance at the clock above the trolley. You pray your father is not back from the factory yet.

As Sister Celina sees you to the door, you find yourself searching for something to say. You notice the ballerina doesn't hurt any more. 'We used to ride the same bus to school,' you say at last. 'Mine was the first stop in the mornings and yours the third, at the banyan. I wanted to tell you, I remembered you.'

She smiles, nods.

You hail the rickshaw just as it is passing by, spokes sounding tinnily. The stationer has closed his shop, so has the tailor, the dhaba is full. Some stores have TV sets turned on. The rickshawala veers slightly to avoid a pothole. The approaching factories, tall chimneys against the night sky, don't seem so lonesome.

MORNING VISITOR

YAMUNA SAT ON THE metal cot, clipping her nails. Her hair was wet. The sun warmed her scalp.

Her two grandsons fenced with wooden swords on the grassless lawn. Amma was doing the dishes in the kitchen which looked on to the veranda. Raju could be heard dusting.

Someone clanked the main gate's latch.

Yamuna glanced up as the gate opened and Pushpa walked in, maroon shawl on one shoulder, jute bag on the other. She went back to clipping her nails.

'How are you?' Pushpa said, settling down on the cot.

'I'm fine.' Her lips twisted as she pared the hard nail of her big toe.

'Is that yours?' Pushpa pointed to the brand-new pistachio Fiat in the veranda.

'Why else would it be parked here?' Yamuna nudged her spectacles up the bridge of her nose. 'We bought it two weeks ago,' she said at last.

'Tch, that's what I was saying, didn't see it here before, no.' She tipped her feet out of the chappals and wiggled her toes.

Raju came out and called to the boys, 'Raghu! Anuj! Come, bhabhi has peeled oranges for you,' then went back in. Behind the cot, a wall-to-wall partition of wood-framed glass doors curtained with muslin separated the inner rooms from the veranda.

'Go now,' Yamuna said, seeing her grandsons still playing. 'And don't eat half and waste the rest. Otherwise see, Auntie is here.' She pointed at Pushpa with her chin while her hands folded the newspaper around the nail parings. 'You know about the dungeon in her house where she puts naughty children, don't you?'

'So?' Pushpa narrowed her eyes. 'Did both of you finish your milk this morning? Come here.'

The boys froze. They gaped at the old woman. Her face was like a shrivelled apricot, her eyes were lined with kohl.

'This bag may look small,' she said, clutching it and shaking her head, 'but it can easily hold ten little shaitans like you.' With an outstretched finger, she pointed at both of them in turn.

The two little boys ran inside the house.

Pushpa, as though reminded of something, started to look through her bag. 'Do you remember Janaki?' she asked Yamuna.

'Who?'

'The one who used to live two lanes away. Back in Lahore. Whose family had a dry fruit shop,' she said, still searching her bag.

'Oh, Janaki! Yes, why?'

'I met her at a client's house last Puranmashi. She turned out to be their relative. I didn't recognize her at first. Then it struck me who she was.' Pushpa looked up. 'And I said, "Remember me? I'm Pushpa. From Lahore." She got up and embraced me with such ardour, Yamuna, I can't tell you.'

Yes, the initial burst of enthusiasm, Yamuna thought. Isn't that why I've had you hanging around my neck for fifteen years now? She will realize her mistake too when she finds you knocking at her door every month.

Yamuna and Pushpa, the two friends, had lost touch in the weeks after Partition when communal violence flared up in Punjab. Like other Hindu and Sikh families, they locked up their ancestral homes and left for the Indian side, carrying only cloth bundles of possessions. Pushpa, her husband and two-year-old son found themselves in the refugee camp at Kingsway in Delhi, while Yamuna and her in-laws went to Kanpur, only later moving to the capital. More than two decades passed without them seeing or hearing from one another. One morning Yamuna was at her tailor's, who worked from his house at a rickety sewing machine set in the courtyard. She was discussing with him the neckline for her kameez when she heard a familiar voice call her name.

Yamuna was elated to see Pushpa, who lived with her family on the first floor. While the tailor watched their beaming faces, his feet working the treadle, fingers guiding the seams, the two friends talked about the old days. Then with sadness, they recounted the story of their journeys from home in what was now Pakistan. They asked after each other's parents and siblings and exchanged notes on their families. How many sons? How many daughters? Pushpa invited her upstairs.

The room was narrow. Its green walls seemed sweaty. Yamuna sat on the charpai, while Pushpa filled her a glass of water from a pitcher in the corner. The window showed the cheap yellow façades of the houses across the lane and clothes spread on lines. Over the cupboard lay a mess of pots and pans, and bundles of clothes that looked like dusty pumpkins. The ropes of the charpai cut into Yamuna's hips. She cleared her throat and shifted her weight. She told Pushpa about their other friend, Radha, who was in Delhi too. Then casually, she asked about Pushpa's means. Pushpa told her that the family was doing well. She spoke about her own job as if it were a pastime, and Yamuna nodded along. She stayed until after lunch.

A month later Pushpa paid Yamuna a visit, followed by a second visit the next month, and one the month after that, each loosely timed to fall on days when people were likely to give donations to brahmins. Yamuna too would give her some money.

Over time the visits started to coincide more and more perfectly with such days. Sometimes she brought along Yamuna's stitched clothes from the tailor.

Yamuna started to avoid her. If she happened to see Pushpa coming through the gate, she would order the cook to tell her she was not at home and send her away. But next month she would find Pushpa clanking the latch again.

Now Pushpa said, 'Janaki asked about you as well. She took your phone number from me and gave hers for you. Here.' She handed Yamuna the chit that she had finally dug out of her bag.

Yamuna looked at the number. 'Where in Delhi?'

'Kamla Nagar. What a house she has, Yamuna! Complete with a white marble temple. So many servants and maids. She has a bell by her bedside, she rings it and a maid comes running in to take orders. Big industrialists her sons have become. Two flour mills, one in Okhla, another one in Haryana. And do you know...'

Twirling her long gold chain, Yamuna listened with interest. These titbits about common acquaintances, and sometimes even about strangers, were the only things that she liked about Pushpa's visits. Whose son or daughter was getting married, who got a car as dowry and who a washing machine, births and deaths, family disputes – Pushpa had all the details.

'I'm going to her house again next month. Why don't I come here and we go together. In your new motorcar, hmm?'

'We'll see,' Yamuna said.

'I'll call you before I come next time.' Pushpa made another try.

Yamuna did not reply.

The two sat in silence, one filing the uneven edge of a nail, the other picking lint off her fleecy shawl.

'I went to Radha's a few days ago,' Pushpa began.

'How is she?' Yamuna put aside the nail clipper.

'She's fine, doing well. Somehow we got reminiscing about old times. Do you remember, Yamuna, how we would sneak into Radha's aunt's room whenever she was out? How we would go through her trunk? And one day she came back earlier than we had expected. You were prancing around the room in her sequin sari. Purple, wasn't it? I had her salwar kameez on. And Radha was doing a song and dance, twirling her aunt's dupatta. What a sound thrashing she gave us!' Pushpa stretched the sentence, relishing it and smiling. Around her eyes the crow's feet crinkled deep.

Yamuna watched her quietly.

'But you know,' Pushpa said, 'whenever I see Radha, I wonder at how she has changed. She was never interested in dressing up or doing her hair. She didn't know a thing about it. And now, always gracefully dressed. Remember, you and I would be putting laces to our saris and dupattas, and she, her hair in tangles, her sari a mess, would be skipping rope in the sun. And this was when we were quite grown-up, no longer little girls.' Yamuna and Pushpa with their fair skins had never considered the darker Radha as pretty as themselves. They treated her offhandedly, and sometimes kept her out of their games and secrets.

'Don't talk rubbish,' Yamuna said. After Radha's marriage into a sophisticated family, she had warmed to her.

'Tch, she herself says that it was her sisters-in-law who groomed her,' Pushpa said. 'Anyway, when I got up to leave, she gave me fifty rupees for Ekadashi and a brand-new shawl.'

Yamuna knew this to be a lie. At the most she would have received a worn shawl along with the usual fifteen or twenty rupees.

'And how many times I've asked you for a sari, and not even a new one at that. Can't you give your friend one sari?' Pushpa continued.

Yamuna shrugged her plump shoulders. 'I didn't get a chance to look through my cupboard. Next time.'

'Next time, next time, same answer you give me always. Then—'

Their conversation was interrupted as Meera, Yamuna's elder daughter-in-law, came out of the house. 'Namaste, Auntie,' she greeted Pushpa.

'Namaste, my daughter. How are you doing?' She dipped into her bag, took out a pair of hand-knitted cream booties and a hat and passed them to her. 'Here, is this what you wanted?'

Meera stretched one little bootie over her fingers to see the design.

Pushpa pointed to Meera's pregnant belly. 'Looks like it'll be a boy again.'

'I'm hoping for a girl this time, Auntie.'

Pushpa smiled. 'Yes, why not.'

'Auntie, do you know how to knit a blouse? My mother wants one. Her eyes have become weak, she doesn't knit any more.'

Pushpa nodded.

'And how much for these?' Meera brushed her hand over the booties and hat.

'Twenty-five.'

'I'll just bring it. Will you have tea?'

'Not at this hour.' Pushpa raised her eyes to the pale blue sky. 'Something else perhaps.'

'I'll send some kanji.'

After Meera went to the kitchen, Pushpa said to Yamuna, 'I have to go get my husband's medicine tomorrow. I'll also get a tin box of this kohl I wear. For Meera's mother. It improves the eyesight.'

'Whose medicine? Your husband's?' Last Yamuna had heard, Pushpa and her husband had not been speaking. 'Are you two back on talking terms then?'

Pushpa shook her head. 'That's not going to happen, at least not in this lifetime. And I hope I don't get saddled with him in the next one,' she added quickly. 'My dharma is to take care of him if he's not well and needs me, and that I do. Nothing more, nothing less.'

'Oh.' Yamuna gathered her hair and did it in a knot. 'It must be strange to live in the same house and not talk to each other?'

'It's gone on for so long, Yamuna, now it doesn't even occur to me as strange. He was the one who built this wall of silence. But now I say, good, very good that he did. Twenty years of blissful peace it has been.'

'He must say the same thing: twenty years of blissful peace, spared of your nonstop chatter.' Yamuna laughed.

'Chatter?' Pushpa looked at her friend. 'I was hardly myself around him. And he for his part preferred to talk with his hands and feet. In the evening the clock would strike six and my heart would go cold. So much beating, so much fault-finding. Educated, manager in a big dry-clean company – is that how they behave!'

Yamuna remained quiet. She had heard this many times.

'But the day I returned his one slap with two tight ones – a year's resolve had gone into those slaps, Yamuna – he understood not to lay a finger on me any more.' Pushpa's face turned red. Sometimes, however, she liked to talk about the years when she used to send her petticoats, even blouses, to the factory for cleaning.

Raju came out with two glasses of kanji. He placed the tray between them. Mustard seeds swam in the purple drink, dark carrot wedges sat at the bottom.

Yamuna took a sip. 'That was when your husband cut himself off from you?'

'Yes, but not immediately. For a month or so we remained on talking terms.' Pushpa paused as though going over that time in her head. 'Then slowly, he stopped speaking with me. I tried to talk, but he would not reply. One evening he returned with a new stove. Took half the utensils and made his separate kitchen in the corner. Next month he didn't give me allowance for my ration, and I didn't go begging to him for any either. "Why should I?" I thought to myself. "Hasn't God given me two hands and legs too? I'll put them to use." Sure there are hard days even now, Yamuna. But I'll survive. Somehow.' Pushpa smiled.

Yamuna looked at her. How does she not crumble, she wondered.

It had been a harsh life. Uneducated, untrained, unprepared to earn a living, Pushpa had found herself thrust out into the world. She started sewing and knitting for the neighbours. It brought in some money, which would have sufficed had her son been earning something too, but he was already on the road to becoming an alcoholic.

Back in Lahore, one of Pushpa's aunts, a poor brahmin widow, had lived on the meals provided by two households in the neighbourhood. She would go round to the houses at noon and again in the evening to collect her meals. On solar and lunar eclipses she even received clothes. Most households followed this contractual tradition. One day Pushpa met an acquaintance who complained of the near absence of such customs in Delhi. She asked Pushpa hesitatingly, for she knew Pushpa's husband was reasonably well off, if she would accept a token donation from her household once in a while. Gradually, one contact led to another, and Pushpa garnered a clientele. It was 1980 now, and she went all over the city on foot, in a rickshaw, by bus. She took whatever the clients gave, little, much, food, money. In return, the clients earned good karma.

Yamuna put her glass back in the tray. Pushpa sat crunching a carrot wedge, eyes closed, the sun knocking at the lids.

Yamuna looked over the side of the cot. 'Amma, where did Raju put the methi leaves? I told him to keep them here,' she called.

Amma was on the lawn hanging washed clothes to dry. 'One minute.' Averting her face, she shook water out of a checked shirt and draped it over the line.

'My knees have started hurting too much. Can't walk,' Yamuna said to Pushpa as their fingers plucked the methi leaves. They dropped the leaves on a newspaper between them and the stalks on a plate.

'Hmm, knee aches tend to get worse in winters. And then the age factor does its bit too.' Pushpa lifted her eyes to look at Yamuna.

'What age factor?' Yamuna asked without a change in expression. She knew well where the conversation was headed. 'Why? You're still okay.'

'Well, I still have some catching up to do there,' Pushpa replied.

'What catching up? We are the same age.'

'You should ask your sister Kanta. She'll tell you. She and I are the same age.'

'How's that possible?' Yamuna looked over her glasses. 'Weren't we in the same class at school?'

'That's because you all started school late.'

'Nonsense,' Yamuna declared, throwing a handful of the separated leaves on the newspaper.

Pushpa lapsed into silence.

Meera returned with three ten-rupee notes. 'Auntie, twenty-five for the booties and hat, and you can keep the five.'

Pushpa clutched the notes. 'I'll make the blouse soon.'

'Navy blue, if you can find the wool,' Meera said before going back in.

'I've been putting off buying garam masala,' Pushpa said to Yamuna. 'I'll buy some on my way back today.' She put the notes in her pouch and tucked it back into her blouse. 'I miss it in my gobi aloo. They just don't taste good without it. Old habits, I guess.' She sighed.

Yamuna nodded. 'It's been so many years, but I'm yet to see a better stocked kitchen than your mother's.'

Pushpa smiled.

'From sweets to sherbets to ten types of pickles. And she loved to feed people,' Yamuna said.

'She was very fond of you. She would say, "I love to see Yamuna eat. How she savours every bite."'

'There were times, Pushpa, when the only reason I could get through the meals at my house was because I knew I would soon be eating something good at yours.'

Yamuna's grandsons rushed past the cot to the far end of the veranda, swords in hand, wearing Rama and Ravana masks this time.

'But all that went away with my father,' Pushpa said. 'He was a good man.'

'You know, even as a child what really struck me about him was that he didn't mind having so many daughters, you were seven sisters after all. But I never heard him complain.'

'Never,' Pushpa echoed. 'Instead, he used to say, "Seven daughters, so what? What trouble do they cause me? As to finding them good husbands and households, they've each come with a prewritten kismat. It will provide accordingly."'

'Hmm, he used to say that, didn't he? I remember now.' Yamuna's eyes drifted away from her friend's face to watch the two boys dance and clack their swords and chase each other around the Fiat, reminding her of her own childhood.

'Your husband's death anniversary must be round the corner,' Pushpa said.

Yamuna turned to look at her. 'Yes. Next Friday. Be here at nine sharp.' Yamuna would wake up early that day to prepare a breakfast of puri, bhaji, raita and kheer that would be served to Pushpa, so that Yamuna's husband would gain merit in the afterlife. After the meal, Pushpa would be given twenty rupees and a new blanket.

'I'll be on time,' Pushpa said.

Through with the methi, Yamuna wrapped the newspaper around the leaves.

'Is it lunchtime already?' Pushpa said, as Raju passed by carrying a stack of plates and bowls.

Yamuna turned to see. 'Hmm, must be one o'clock.'

Pushpa waited for a minute, then said, 'I think I'll go.' She gathered her bag, slipped on her chappals and got up. 'My Puranmashi dakshina?' she asked, wrapping the maroon shawl around her.

'Yes.' Yamuna patted the front of her blouse. Locating a tenner and two fivers folded in it, she took them out. Since Meera had already given her five rupees, she had made up her mind to give only another fifteen to Pushpa instead of the usual twenty. But at the last minute she decided against it. 'Here.' She handed her all three notes.

Pushpa put her palms together. 'Namaste.'

Yamuna watched Pushpa's shawled back recede, her lizard of a plait hanging over it. It was perhaps Pushpa's kismat that she be poor, have the husband she had, that her friends become her patrons, rich women with cars and bungalows who held her in disdain. In her next life, she hoped, her friend would start a new account. The latch clicked into place. Pushpa's shrivelled face appeared above it. Then she turned and left.

Yamuna sat there on the cot a while longer.

OTHER SIDE OF TOWN

JOHNNY WALKER'S THOUGHTS DRIFTED back to Rani, and for a moment he stopped massaging Madan's legs. Madan groaned, tapped him with his foot to continue. Johnny Walker took some oil and rubbed it into the legs. He glanced at the clock.

Nirmal sat on her side of the bed, plaiting her hair. All day she had noticed Johnny Walker's lack of attention, his restlessness. It was there when he ironed the clothes. It was there when he kneaded the dough, adding flour, then water, then more flour, then water.

'Go now, sleep,' she said.

He picked up the bottle of oil, moved the air cooler closer to the bed and left.

Lying in his room on the terrace, he pictured how he had run into Rani that morning as she walked up the lane pushing a garbage cart. He asked her about the fire on her side of town. The sun was hot and they went to stand on the shaded side. He asked how long the fire truck took to arrive, but Rani was surveying the grilled windows of the house across the road. He thought that odd, but before he could think more, she kissed him.

He folded his arms under his head. A lone bulb lit his room, the table fan droned. He went over the scene again. How it had happened. How her lips were apart already when she kissed him. The heat of her breath. The sudden awareness of their saliva mingling. The hurt and shame that crossed her face when he pushed her away. She was a low-caste sweeper. What if somebody had seen them? Gossip travelled fast in this small town. How would he have explained himself to Nirmal and Madan? He turned on his side, making the charpai creak. On the windowsill lay a freckled mirror and a razor, his frayed toothbrush and a tube of Colgate. He had once been close to getting married. Shiv, who worked at the hardware store, had offered the hand of his daughter. The girl was plump, fair, belonged to a good caste, and Nirmal approved of the match. A few weeks before the wedding, however, the girl died of pneumonia. Heartbroken and desperate to get away from the town, he had taken the train to Delhi to visit Nirmal's daughter Meera and her family. At Meera's house he did light chores during the day, and in the evenings stole away to the red-light district. But nothing like what had happened this morning had ever happened before. He traced his lips with his thumb. He shivered, still feeling Rani's warm breath on them.

The sparrows' chirping woke Johnny Walker. He went and stood by the parapet. The sun hadn't broken from the clouds yet. Below, Kapurthala spread like a labyrinth. A milkman cycled through the tight lanes, balancing heavy cans of milk. A red pennant fluttered from a faraway temple top. He took a deep breath and brushed down the creases of his kurta.

Downstairs, while Madan did his morning prayers and Nirmal boiled the milk and prepared the tea, Johnny Walker chopped vegetables for lunch. He dusted the house, starting with the faded maroon and gold brocade sofas and the fake deerskin that hung behind the divan, and then moved from room to room. When Madan set out for his factory, Johnny Walker walked him to the bus stop, carrying the lunchbox. The rest of the morning, he sat in the staircase trying to fix the whistle of an old pressure cooker despite Nirmal telling him to do the laundry.

In the afternoon she retired for her nap, and he stepped out with the grocery bag. He meant to go to the bazaar, but then started towards the far side of town where the poorer section lived. The sun was behind him. Sturdy buffalos stood here and there in the lanes, ruminating. Flies buzzed outside the dispensary and rickshawalas dozed under trees. The town tapered as he walked on, the houses growing more and more cramped and only a storey high.

He knocked at a blue door.

It opened partway, revealing Rani's face. She didn't have a dupatta around her head. Her hair was in a long, thick plait. 'What happened?' she said.

'Nothing.' Over her shoulder, he could see a brown-and-white goat bleating and blinking at him curiously. 'I was passing by and wondered if I could get a glass of water.' He immediately regretted his words. Still, he followed her inside.

He sat on his heels, while Rani went to the kitchen. The narrow courtyard looked recently swept. A fragrance of brick and water rose from it. The goat settled down and lay on its side, tethered to a pole. A charpai leaned against a wall.

Rani brought him a glass of water and sat next to the goat. The goat craned its neck and Rani scratched it. Her dark wrists were bare. They were strong wrists, broad but not thick. In town, she didn't mix with the other sweepers, never stopped to have a cup of tea with them. Each sweeper had a neighbourhood marked out, and it was a tacit agreement not to encroach upon another's turf. Three years ago she started to clean toilets in a house outside her area – the mistress was unhappy with her old sweeper. The sweeper abused Rani in the street, gathering a crowd, accusing her of snatching food from her mouth. Rani spat on the ground and went her way. She now petted the goat's head, gently touching the spots where the horns would come out.

'Does she give milk?' Johnny Walker pointed to the goat with his glass.

'Not yet. Her mother gave ample though. My sister has three children, so I sent the mother with her.'

'I didn't know you had a sister.'

She crossed her arms over her knees. 'Do you have work on this side of town?'

'Yes ... Nirmal sent me to inquire about a cobbler.'

Rani nodded. 'Do you have any brothers or sisters?'

He hadn't thought about them in a long time. No one had asked this question in years. 'I had eight.' He set the glass to one side. 'But I don't know where they are now. I never wrote or went back.'

'Why did you leave?'

'There was never enough to eat. And my old man beat me a lot. After I ran away, I was scared a neighbour or a relative might spot me and give him my whereabouts. So I tried to get further and further away, walking, hitchhiking on trucks, finding work at a tea stall now, a dhaba next. My mother had named me Deenanath. Doesn't suit me, right?' He laughed, revealing his crooked teeth. 'So as soon as I left home, I renamed myself after my favourite comedian. I wanted to go to Bombay, but fate brought me to Kapurthala, and Nirmal and Madan took me in.'

Rani watched his thick lips and the grey hair that fell over his forehead in a thatch. His kurta-pajama that was perhaps once white looked grubby now. She remembered hearing that he was in ragged clothes and resembled a scarecrow when he had first appeared in town some thirty-five years ago.

The sun was melting in the sky. 'I'll go now,' he said. At the door he smiled at her, the heaviness from yesterday having lifted off and his heart light again. He glanced up and down the lane and slipped out.

Rani picked up the glass he had left. She poured the water over the bricks, hurt that he didn't drink it.

JOHNNY WALKER WAS POLISHING the banister when the postman brought a pale envelope with foreign stamps. Johnny Walker took it to Nirmal, who was in her room arranging her cupboard. He sat at the edge of the bed while she read the letter, saris and petticoats in a heap near her feet. Amol, Nirmal's son, lived in America, in a city where it rained all year long. He had started out as a mail boy, and in those early days Johnny Walker would imagine him going from door to door in the rain delivering letters and feel sorry for the poor boy. Sometimes Johnny Walker and Nirmal rode the bus to Madan's factory to talk with Amol over the phone. He was now a manager in the postal services.

'What does he write?'

'He says he's doing well. He's got a green card. He's permanent now, Johnny!'

'Oh good. He's been waiting for it for so long. What else does he say?'

'He asks about you, how you are doing, and sends his love to all of us.'

Johnny Walker smiled and fondly smoothed down the bedsheet. Amol used to bring him a paan in exchange for getting his shoes polished. He had taught Johnny Walker how to ride a scooter and swear in English. He teased him if he caught him chatting up a maid. When Amol's friends came over, the boys got him to do his namesake's drunkard routine. Johnny Walker would lift his shoulders, turn out his palms, totter a little, and deliver a dialogue from *Madhumati*. How they would laugh. The house seemed empty and forlorn with Amol and Meera gone. It brightened only briefly in the summer when Meera visited with Raghu and Kavya.

'Amol wants his father and me to go live with him.' Nirmal laughed. 'But how can we, Johnny? We have a house here, and the factory too. Our whole life is here.' She folded the letter and passed it to him to tuck under her pillow.

The family's sweet shop had been sold years ago. Madan invested the gains in a ball bearing factory. But business had been dipping steadily, and even ten years after the government curbed the Sikh extremists in Operation Blue Star, few wanted to have dealings with a company in Punjab. Clients and orders were hard to come by. Madan was forced to sell off machines that he had sourced with great care. Half the labour was sacked. When Johnny Walker and Nirmal visited the factory, they found Madan sitting in the office reading the paper while a single machine rattled half-heartedly in the background. Madan still ordered for them a lunch of puri chana, but the bottles of Coca-Cola were missing. And when the two were ready to leave, he would close the factory early and take the bus home with them. The driver had been dismissed years ago, followed by the car.

Johnny Walker warmed up the lunch and laid the table. Nirmal asked him to bring the letter from the room. She reread it as she ate.

He poured her a glass of water. 'Amol will propose just anything, you finish your lunch first.'

She nodded but read on.

In the afternoon she sent him to fetch a plumber to fix the kitchen tap. Instead, he went to Rani's.

The blue door was open. Rani sat outside the kitchen darning a kameez, the goat by her side. When she saw him, she laid the charpai and shut the door.

He told her about Amol's letter and how he had asked Nirmal and Madan to come live with him in America. 'They won't go anywhere, I know,' he said, as though Rani was the one who needed this reassurance.

'They won't.' She put her hand on his. He opened his palm to let her fingers slip in. Loyalty, she thought, was a habit. If he was loyal to them, he would be loyal to anyone who was in his life.

JOHNNY WALKER STOPPED AT the sweet shop and asked for half a kilo of barfi. The shop looked the same as it had when

Madan's family owned it, with its flaky green walls and the glass shelf of sweets and savouries. But business was not the same. Madan's father had been famous for his sweets. People still remembered his gulab jamuns, kaju katlis and succulent imartis. The present owner sat wearing a vest. Many a time in the past, he had asked Johnny Walker to come work for him, offering to double, triple what Madan paid, even throwing in a bonus for Diwali. He caught a fly hovering over the glass shelf and asked Johnny Walker how he was doing.

The attendant packed the barfi and tied the box with a string. With the packet under his arm, a song on his lips, and a soft rain falling, Johnny Walker sauntered towards Rani's house.

As he knocked at the door though, he wondered if he should have brought the sweets. But he was here and so was the barfi and there was nothing to be done about it.

Rani opened the door and stepped aside. He felt she was expecting him. It hung in the air somehow.

'Where's your goat?' he said, finding the courtyard empty.

'When it rains, she goes into my room and refuses to come out. Her name's Lata.'

They sat outside the bedroom where the roof jutted a little, so that they would be saved from the drops. The dust-coloured sky hung low with clouds. There was a patch of orange rain under the street lamp.

He gave her the box of sweets.

She smiled and tugged at the string to untie it. They took a piece of barfi each. But as she bit into it, she remembered how he would not drink the water from her kitchen.

The house and the town beyond were silent. The rain fell in big drops.

'Do you not feel lonely, living by yourself?' he said.

'I have Lata.' She fiddled with her anklet, straightening its bells. 'When my husband passed away ten years ago and then my mother-in-law, the silence suffocated me. But it's strange how it grows on you and almost becomes a presence, someone you can talk to, pass your time with.'

He pictured her in the house, late in the evenings, turning on the lights, moving from the room to the kitchen to the courtyard, folding the washing, chopping vegetables, and the silence following her around.

'I can't imagine living alone.'

'When my husband wasn't obsessing with water, bathing five times a day as though he were a brahmin, or washing his clothes in the middle of the night, he went to a woman. I can't say I miss that too much.'

'Some said he was possessed by a spirit. But I think there were just some screws loose in his head,' Johnny Walker said.

'I could never figure him out. Still, after he passed away, I cried for months.'

'How old were you when he died?'

'It was eight years ago. I must have been twenty-three. Sometimes I wish he had given me a child.' She fiddled with the anklet again. 'But I have Lata. It's okay.'

Johnny Walker kissed her.

When he was heading out, she gave him a polythene bag to cover his head, but they were glad for the rain because no one would see him leaving her house so late.

Now every third or fourth day, Johnny Walker would visit Rani. Her body with its two shades seemed new to him every time they made love, the stomach darker than the breasts, the thighs fairer than the calves. Afterwards he would look at her as she lay by his side, trying to imprint the colour palette of her body on his mind. It disturbed him though when she asked him to leave her a mark on her lips or neck or breasts, something that she could return to when he was away. He would laugh it off, tell her she was being childish. He thought about her constantly when they were apart but never told her so. Rani would bathe in the afternoon on returning from work, smooth her body with mustard oil, put on glass bangles to match her salwar kameez, and wait for Johnny Walker. It pleased him to see her make this effort. Nirmal had got him his first pair of glasses two years ago, and though he used them only when cleaning rice and lentils, he had started to feel old. He couldn't figure what Rani saw in him, why she would desire him. In the evening, before he left, they snacked together in the kitchen. He taught her how to soak a slice of bread in sweet milk and shallow fry it, like

Nirmal, or make his favourite besan ka chilla. Rani looked forward to this half an hour as much as the lovemaking. He moved with ease through her house now, in and out of the kitchen, or lounged in the narrow courtyard with Lata blinking sedately. One day he bought an exhaust fan for the kitchen and put a twenty-rupee note in Rani's palm to send for the electrician later. When she folded her fingers over the note, it quietly changed something between them. Johnny Walker had never known what it was to be a part of a house or someone's life in this way.

'WHERE WERE YOU THE whole afternoon and evening?' Nirmal asked as she sat in the cane chair in the kitchen with her tea. She was familiar with Johnny Walker's habit of lingering in the bazaars, chatting with shopkeepers, stopping five minutes here and ten there. He knew practically the whole town and it him. But these long spells of disappearance over the past few months were new.

'I sat down to watch a few scenes from *Mere Mehboob* in Kishan's shop and two hours just flew by.' He laughed. He was chopping a cauliflower, cross-legged on the floor.

'Does he have a VCR?'

Johnny Walker nodded.

She put some namkeen in her mouth and munched it slowly. Something had changed about him, but she couldn't say what. 'Is that oil in your hair?'

'Yes.' He flattened down the hair on to his forehead. 'It was very dry. Why? Does it not look good?'

'It's all right.'

She warmed her hands around the teacup. The weather was turning, the days growing cooler and shorter. The white light of the tube reflected off the blue kitchen walls. 'We are going to America,' she said. They were moving permanently, but she didn't want to tell him this, so she added, 'For six months, Johnny.'

'What? You never told me!' He had felt something was up, but he was too absorbed with Rani to have paid attention. Nirmal and Madan indeed had been whispering amongst themselves for weeks now, buzzing with barely suppressed excitement. He assumed they were fixing Amol's marriage, though a couple of times he worried they had found out about him and Rani. Last night too, they fell quiet when he brought them gajar ka halwa in bed, and the moment he left the room, the murmuring picked up again.

'But I'm telling you now. Amol has been insisting, Johnny. He's been there by himself for so many years, I think he's lonely. He wants us to go live with him.'

'Can't he come down during the holidays instead? Six months is too long.'

'This time he wants us to visit.'

'But you'll not like it in America.' He shook his head, deliberating over what to say. 'It will be very cold.' In winter

Nirmal slept with a woollen scarf around her head, and before retiring to his room Johnny Walker would tuck a hot-water bottle under her feet.

'The houses are warm there,' she said. 'One doesn't even need a sweater indoors.'

Johnny Walker plucked a green worm that stuck to the stem and put it with the waste. 'You'll not like it. You'll see ... Amol told me everyone speaks English there.'

This worried Nirmal too, but Madan was so set on starting a new life in America that she didn't want to dampen his spirits with her anxiety. He was arranging to sell the factory and they were going to rent out the house as well. He had already ordered Lovely Tailors to stitch them a warm coat each.

'What about me?' Johnny Walker said at last.

She got up and placed the namkeen jar in the overhead cabinet. They had arranged for him to work for Meera's family in Delhi – who planned to use him as a watchman in the factory – with the understanding that if Nirmal and Madan ever returned, they could have him back. But they didn't need to tell him all this, not yet, perhaps not until the last moment when the three of them were in Delhi, Madan had said.

'What about me, Nirmal Didi?' he pressed.

'Umm ... You'll take care of this house while we are gone,' she said from behind the cabinet door.

He sighed and returned to chopping the cauliflower.

She set the cup in the sink. 'I'll send you a watch, Johnny. A nice one with a leather strap.'

'HOW ARE YOU?' JOHNNY Walker said to Rani. She was feeding Lata vegetable peelings. He hadn't seen her in ten days, except for a brief visit one evening. Nirmal had suddenly announced she wanted to clear out all old and unnecessary things, and they were spending the afternoons sifting through clothes, bed linen, utensils, books, shoes, old calendars, knitting needles, embroidery hoops, everything that she had accumulated over the past forty years. Johnny Walker's body ached from the work. He rolled his shoulders now, and they made a popping sound.

'What's this?' Rani pointed to the polythene bag in his hand.

'See for yourself.'

In the bag was a yellow phulkari dupatta. 'It's beautiful. Such colourful embroidery. But why is it warm?' she said, bunching the fabric in her fingers.

He laughed. He had got it ironed on the way. 'Nirmal was going to throw it out, but when she wasn't looking, I picked it up for you.'

'Oh.' She rolled the dupatta and dropped it back into the bag. 'Come, have lunch.'

Lata, done with the peelings, pressed herself against Johnny Walker's legs. He stroked her. 'But are you not going to try it? I want to see how it looks on you.'

'Later.'

He followed her to the kitchen. She served sabzi and chapati, and spooned some pickle on to his plate. He looked at her in between bites, wanting to say this or that, but she seemed focused on her food. She didn't look at him once. When they went to the bedroom and lay down for a nap, he said, 'Is it because I didn't come see you?'

She had her back towards him. She reached for his arm and wrapped it around her waist.

He drew her closer. 'I wanted to come.'

'I know.' Then she added, 'Stay the night today.'

'That won't be possible. What will I tell Nirmal and Madan?'

'They don't own you, do they? Or is it that you don't want me to have the slightest claim on you?'

'That's not true.' Sometimes he thought he'd marry her; rent a room in town and settle down with her; leave for work in the morning and return in the evening; or live with her in his room on the terrace. Sometimes it seemed easy. But he knew Nirmal would not let her into the house. And what would Rani do after marriage? He wouldn't want her to continue cleaning people's toilets. He imagined her wilting on the terrace in the heat, and growing bitter and dry and brittle. He slipped her sleeve off her shoulder and rested his forehead against her warm skin. He shut his eyes but couldn't sleep.

Rani was snoring. He shook her lightly. 'After Nirmal and Madan leave for America next week, I'll stay with you the whole six months, or as long as you will let me.'

She turned towards him, sleepy but pleased.

SHIRLEY

HEMA REMOVED TEABAGS FROM the porcelain jar and placed them in the mugs – Mr Clarke's large yellow one, and the beige one with strawberries that she had come to like. On the windowsill were the dahlias she had watered this morning, the first thing she did when she came in. She had learned to take off her shoes and leave them on the rack next to Mr Clarke's tassel loafers, and pad around the house barefoot. Mr Clarke wore mouse-coloured socks. She could see him now, sitting in his armchair, peering at the book with a magnifying glass, the table lamp focused on the page. On the days she came over and after they had had lunch, the two sat in the living room with William Trevor's *Collected Stories*, a gift from his niece three years ago. 'Happy Birthday, Uncle John. July 1993' was inscribed inside the cover in large block letters – back then, he told her, he could still see bold scripts. Hema would turn to the contents and read out the titles, and he would pick a story for the afternoon. Today they were reading 'Lunch in Winter'.

She brought the tea to the living room, placed Mr Clarke's mug in his hands and settled on the sofa across from him.

'I was wondering, my dear, if next week you could help me write out some Christmas cards?'

'Sure, Mr Clarke.'

He smoothed down the striped throw over his lap. He sipped at his mug. It must be strange to be seen and not see, Hema thought. From what she had understood in the interview, she must appear to him as a blurred shadow on the sofa, while he sat there fully visible in his red sweater, which he wore every day without fail.

'You must think, Christmas is still months away, why do the cards now? I like getting them ready in advance, dear, lest I forget. Anna was particular about these things, and I don't want to break with tradition.' He laughed, and Hema knew he was going to recount something from his past. 'You know, when I was captured by the Germans, the British army thought I was dead and sent Anna my death notice. She said she didn't believe it for a second, but she kept the letter her whole life.' He felt for the photo frame on the side table, which held a black-and-white picture of Anna and him.

'How were the Germans, Mr Clarke? I mean, were they cruel? Did they ill-treat the prisoners?'

'No, they weren't cruel, though that was mainly on account of the Geneva Convention. They made us work long hours in potato fields, but at least it ensured there was always food to eat. I'll have Lisa look for the letter next time she comes down, so I can show it to you.'

Hema smiled. She opened the book and resumed reading, enunciating every word as best she could. She sipped the tea in between paragraphs. She hadn't heard of or read Trevor before coming to England, but she found she liked him. As she began to lose herself in the narrative, she felt like folding her legs on the sofa but refrained.

It was four by the time they came to the end of the story. Hema made a mark next to the title on the contents page and returned the book to its place on the shelf between Henry Green's *Loving* and V.S. Pritchett's *Collected Stories*. Mr Clarke shuffled over to the console and turned on the radio. She cleared the mugs.

'I'll go now,' she said. 'See you on Friday.'

'Yes, dear. And please take your cheque.' He pointed towards a white envelope on the table, one of the dozen Hema had bought last week, along with staples and glue. 'Let me know when it clears.'

Outside, Hema slid the cheque from the envelope. The sky was overcast. A cold breeze blew. She looked at her name written in Mr Clarke's oversized handwriting. *I'm tempted not to cash it, Shirley. My first paycheque.* She wanted to hug it to her chest. *I worked for a month and there I was, holding my salary. The world never felt so fair.* The wind flapped against her sari, making the fabric stick between her legs, like trousers. She started down Earlham Road towards the bus stop, composing the letter in her head.

THEY TURNED LEFT FROM Panchkuian on to a quiet, tree-lined avenue, an odd car, a motorcyclist whizzing by. Shirley pulled up opposite Birla Mandir. 'You should drive,' she said, and climbed out of the car.

Hema watched her circle the Maruti and appear at her window.

'Come on.'

'But Shirley, I don't know how to drive.'

'Yes, and that's why you should learn.' She opened the door. 'Come on. You only need to take us to the end of the road.' Her cheeks bore acne scars that showed pink against her dark skin. A silver cross glinted in the open collar of her shirt.

Hema stepped out reluctantly, and they switched seats.

'So that's the accelerator.' Shirley pointed to one of the three pedals in the seat well. 'That's the brake. And this is the clutch. Next I'll tell you how to shift gears.' Hema listened. A car passed by outside, then two cyclists with a long ladder between them. 'Now hold the clutch down and put the car in first gear.'

'Are you sure?'

'Yes, go on.'

Hema was nervous but also excited to be behind the wheel. She pressed down on the clutch, put the car in gear, and slowly released the pedal as Shirley had explained. The car lurched. She glanced at Shirley. It felt like the car was going to shudder to a stop, but just then it gave a big hiccup and rolled forward.

'Second gear.' Shirley put her hand on Hema's and shifted the stick. Hema tried to memorize the movement.

They laughed when she finally managed to overtake the labouring cyclists; it felt like a victory, the car in third gear! Other than Shirley, Hema didn't know any woman who drove, and Shirley was as skilful as any man. Today she had honked two DTC buses out of the way. She had invited Hema this morning to the annual flower show at Roshanara. At the club, they wandered through the display of tulips, sunflowers, roses, colourful cacti, then stopped for lunch at the dining hall. Shirley and her husband were long-time members of the club. Hema imagined them drinking sherry here on Sunday evenings and dancing to live jazz. She pictured a life fuller than her own. Shirley scanned the menu. Hema gazed out of the French windows at the club's wide, green lawns. After lunch when the two were ready to leave, Shirley offered her a lift to Talkatora.

Hema honked.

'Relax. That car's still a kilometre away.'

Hema readjusted her grip on the wheel. She was sitting stiffly, almost leaning over the steering, but she couldn't help her posture. 'Do you think I can stop close to those autorickshaws?'

'Okay, steer left. Now apply the brakes gently.'

Hema hit the brakes and the car came to a sudden stop, cutting off the engine.

'Don't worry. You did well.'

'You think so?'

She nodded.

'But Shirley, I don't understand. What's the point? I don't even have a car.'

'If you know how to drive, maybe you'll buy a car someday. Who knows ... Go now, ask one of the autos if it will take you home.'

'Thank you, Shirley.' It was a new friendship, but Hema had a feeling it would endure.

She boarded an auto and Shirley drove off, waving to her from the open window.

'I DIDN'T KNOW WE could just walk on to the campus,' Sanjay said.

'Mr Clarke and his wife came here sometimes, he told me. He said the university has a "no fence" policy.' They strolled around the broad, its water green, placid, and the area surrounded by trees and bushes. A boy and a girl, students perhaps, passed by jogging. An unshaven man sat by the bank with his fishing gear. The day was clear but chilly. Nature was slowly turning to colours of brown and rust; as a result, everything looked crisp. 'I'm afraid it's going to get terribly cold soon,' Hema said.

'It should be okay. We'll manage.' It was Sanjay's habit to walk with his hands in his pockets, looking straight ahead. He had wanted to come to England since he was ten, when he had seen his uncle at the Indira Gandhi Airport amidst his suitcases with a greatcoat over his arm. Sanjay dwelt on the coat and its rich fur collar whenever he recalled the vision, so Hema knew he was looking forward to winter. She rubbed her palms together. She wished there was a cosy petticoat that she could wear under her sari.

Round the bend, on the shallow side, they came upon a woman standing arms akimbo, watching her dog swim towards a floating stick. Hema and Sanjay too stopped to watch. The dog retrieved the stick and waded back to the woman, nostrils flaring, puffing out clouds. The woman threw the stick in again. The dog leapt after it. Hema liked Norwich with its quiet life and fresh air. Here she had a house of her own for the first time, a desk, a job. Sanjay had insisted on accompanying her to the interview with Mr Clarke to ascertain whether she would be safe spending the day alone with him at his house, and she had let him. In Delhi he would have never agreed to her taking up a job, though to be fair she had never tried.

'Come.' He tapped her arm.

Hema looked at him and was reminded that last week he had shaved off his moustache. Stepping out of the bathroom, running the towel over his freshly shaved lips and cheeks, he had said the moustache was out of place in England. He seemed younger now, even vulnerable. *It's almost like kissing a new man,* Hema had written to Shirley, hoping to make her smile. She imagined her in her printed kaftan, reading the letter in bed, eyelids swollen, pink veins showing, the room unkempt, dust gathering on every surface. *I've started going for a walk in the evening,* Shirley wrote. *It gives shape to my day, which otherwise feels long and unending. I'm thinking of returning to my job, but I'm not sure yet. Join a course, Shirley,* Hema meant to write back, *take it easy for a while. I remember you mentioning once that you want to learn the piano.*

Through a clearing they glimpsed the concrete, ziggurat-like structure of the school building.

'It's a bit ugly, isn't it? I was expecting something old, something grand,' Sanjay said.

'Yes, I see what you mean ... There's a museum on the campus though. Do you want to go have a look?'

'Another time, maybe.'

They walked, crushing dry leaves underfoot.

'Don't they sound like papads?' Hema said.

They listened to the crunching leaves.

'LET'S STAY HERE FOR a while. Or do you need to head back?' Shirley held under her arm the copy of *Gora* that she had checked out on Hema's recommendation.

'I prepared dal and sabzi before leaving, so it's okay, I can stay.'

They sat down on the steps outside the library. Shirley reclined, leaning her elbows on the step above.

'Parrots,' she said, as a bunch of birds sprang out of a nearby tree and flew across the fading sky.

'How can you tell?'

'By their tails. See how long and pointy they are.'

They watched the birds, their tails like nail files.

'My Auntie Perth had a parrot. She called it Cuckoo.' Shirley looked at Hema and they laughed. Shirley wore a gypsy skirt with a black waistband. 'Auntie Perth also had a good-looking tenant. Peter. He was the first boy I kissed. I would go to Auntie's every afternoon under the pretext of learning to bake. At four, Peter would return from the university and we would have a long, lingering kiss under the stairs.'

'How old were you?'

'Eleven perhaps.'

'That's young. Priya is eleven.' Hema didn't want to sound judgemental. She liked Shirley's free spirit.

'Maybe, but what can we do now. At least he kissed well.' She winked.

The gardener turned on the hose and sat on his haunches to water the tall grass. The library was single-storeyed and looked more like a decrepit bungalow. Inside, the walls were pale, and the librarian, a small man, stamped the books loudly in red ink. Hema and Shirley had met here for the first time weeks ago in the aisle between bookracks, while Hema was deliberating over *Punin and Baburin*.

'Francis won't be home for two hours, and I don't want to spend the evening alone editing commas and apostrophes.' Shirley leafed through *Gora*. 'What do you do when you are not reading? Don't you get bored at home?'

'Sometimes, yes, but there are always things to do around the house. And then, once a week I come to the library.' Hema generally would not say more, but she knew it would interest Shirley, and so she added, 'I like to write too. A couple of hours every day, I do that.'

Shirley looked up from the book. 'What do you write?'

'Stories.'

'Short stories?'

'Yes.' It grew dark and the gardener turned on the bulb. Hema watched mosquitoes hover over Shirley's head.

'Which language do you write in? Hindi, Punjabi ... or English?'

'English.'

'That's interesting. And where are the stories set? Don't mind my questions, Hema, I'm just curious.'

'No, not at all. Most of them are set in Kapurthala, in Punjab, where I grew up.' She told Shirley about the small town and its tight bazaars, the joint family living in a large, rambling house, her aunt's collection of English novels from which she lent her one book at a time, the late-night Ramayana recitals she would go to with her mother, and her parents' deaths soon after her marriage. When the librarian came out with a padlock and secured the door, the two got up to go home.

'Have you had anything published?'

Hema smiled. 'Of course not. I'm not that good.'

'I wrote stories too when I was in college, but I could never finish them. They just went on and on.'

'Maybe you were writing a novel.'

Shirley rolled her eyes. 'Anyway. Do you want to practise?' She dropped the car keys in Hema's palm.

HEMA RINSED THE PLATES and stood them on the rack to dry. She sprinkled soap on the carrots and peas that stuck to the bottom of the pan, and let it soak. Through the net curtains she could see the road. She had grown used to the view, but today the way sunlight broke through clouds and fell upon the row of identical brick houses and the plane trees that flanked the road suddenly reminded her that she was in England. It thrilled and scared her to think how far she had come and how much she had left behind. Delhi, the house she shared with her in-laws, the crumbling library, Shirley, her books. All she had managed to squeeze into the bags was a slim collection of Amrita Pritam's stories. She scrubbed the pan. A clump of snow glinted on the sidewalk. Most of it had melted in the last few days. She had been knitting in the living room when snow the size of cotton balls started to float down outside the window. She and Priya quickly slipped on their coats and went out. *I couldn't have imagined snow to be so soft and flaky and yet to creak under my feet,* she wrote to Shirley. *All those Russian novels had led me to understand it as thick layers and sheets. Perhaps books don't have the power to completely or exactly translate life. Anyhow, the snow is beautiful; it makes the nights look bright. But it's tricky to walk on. See, no book ever told me you could slip on snow. Hema,* Shirley wrote back, *I hope you are not going around in that weather in your cotton saris. Your mother-in-law is 6,000 km away. She cannot see you.*

'Shall we go, Mummy?' Priya appeared in the doorway.

'Yes.' Hema wiped the sides of the sink and spread the washcloth on the counter to dry.

Outside, halfway down the street, Miss Jello joined them. She was fat and yellow and swished her tail as she walked.

'She always knows when we leave the house,' Priya said.

'Yes, and these past few days she's been walking me back from the stop too.' They had christened the cat Miss Jello after the way Sanjay's mother pronounced 'yellow'. It looked like she belonged to one of the neighbours, but they couldn't tell which one.

At the stop, Miss Jello sat in a triangle of sunlight while Hema consulted the timetable and Priya settled on the bench. Priya took out her rose lip balm and applied it to her lips with her little finger. She had a slim face and beautiful curly hair. Hema watched as she rubbed her lips together. Mr Clarke had dozed off after lunch last week, and she had tucked her feet under her on the sofa and read 'Nice Day at School'. Disturbed by the story, she had refused Priya permission for a sleepover, causing a weekend-long sulk that only ended this morning. Priya offered her the lip balm. Hema shook her head. When the bus arrived, Miss Jello slunk away through a gap in the hedge.

They rode through narrow streets towards the city centre, passing houses with red, green or blue doors, Tesco, a florist and Tim's Fish and Chips. Hema pointed out Mr Clarke's house with its bay window and dried-up ivy.

'How do you like her jeans?' Priya slanted her head towards a woman in the aisle.

'They're nice.'

'I think we should try and find a similar pair for you ... I can't wait to see you in jeans.' She squeezed her mother's hand.

Hema pressed her daughter's thin, long fingers to her lips. When the bus stopped at the large cathedral on Unthank Road, she said, 'Priya, we should spend a day together sightseeing.' So far they had only visited the marketplace for clothes, supplies, second-hand books, or ambled through the cobblestone lanes looking into shop windows, ending the excursion at the sweetshop where they bought Maltesers, Fruit Pastilles and all the candies they had read about but never tried. Hema saved some to nibble at her desk while writing. Someone pressed the bell and the bus halted at the next stop. A man in a beret got off. A woman boarded with a stroller. The baby wore mitts and a cap and had apple-red cheeks. A young man in the front offered the woman his seat. Hema looked out of the window. Shirley had started learning French at Alliance Française. *The class is thrice a week. It's not very interesting, but I like the distraction. It's nice to have somewhere to go to. I was hoping to make new friends, but the students are young, most of them college-going, and the teacher is a potbellied man with six fingers, Mr Reddy. You can imagine his accent.* Shirley was trying hard to get back on her feet, to once again engage with life, and Hema felt sad about having left her at a time when she needed a friend. The bus turned left and hurtled past the Nestlé factory. Hema and Priya got off at Castle Hill. The day was growing grey. Clouds were gathering.

'I REALLY WANT TO see a play sometime,' Hema said to Shirley. She stuffed the golgappa into her mouth. Shri Ram Centre wasn't far from where they stood, Kamani Auditorium was close by too, and the proximity to the theatres lent the small market an artistic air.

'We can go to Kamani and check if they have anything scheduled for this evening.' Shirley drank up the jaljeera and dabbed her mouth with a handkerchief.

'I don't mean right now.'

'Why not? Sometimes you should do things on the spur of the moment. Let's go.' She pulled her by the arm. Hema barely managed to set the plate and money on the counter. Coins crashed to the floor. She glanced back at the shopkeeper apologetically.

They walked down Tansen Marg with long, quick steps. The amaltas trees were bright yellow against the mauve sky; cars were turning on their headlights; a plastic bag cartwheeled down the road. The evening suddenly seemed full of possibilities.

'I read your story, by the way.' Shirley pulled out the handwritten sheets from her purse and returned them to Hema.

'What did you think?'

'Halfway through, I forgot that you'd written it. It felt like I was reading a book.'

'Really?' Hema couldn't help but smile.

'I've never been to Punjab, but I got a sense of that place from your story. It's just in the background, but it's there.'

They crossed the roundabout to reach Copernicus Marg. Hema told her about Amrita Pritam and her stories, 'Shah di Kanjari' in particular, which was her favourite. Shirley hadn't read the Punjabi author, and when she suggested Hema translate her works to English, Hema's eyes lit up. They reached the auditorium discussing the scope and potential of such a project.

Abhimanyu, two hours long, was slated for the evening. People stood in the foyer talking in hushed voices, waiting for the play to start.

'It will be late by the time we get back home, and I haven't even told Sanjay.'

'You can call him now.' Shirley pointed to the payphone.

As Hema dialled the number, Shirley whispered, 'Tell your husband I'll drop you back.'

Sanjay was saying she could stay – Hema nodded to let Shirley know. She hung up and they rushed to the ticket booth. 'See, all you need to do is try,' Shirley said.

The lights were dim when they entered the theatre. They shuffled to their seats holding hands. Three singers in colourful Rajasthani turbans sat to one side of the stage, singing the story of how the Pandavas came to fight the Kauravas in the battle of Kurukshetra. Their gravelly voices and the energy of a live performance gave Hema goosebumps. She rubbed her arms. The singers recited the episode where Arjuna, lying in bed one evening with Subhadra, described to her the circular, military formation of a chakravyuha. Arjuna was trying to impress his pregnant wife, but Subhadra, bored, stifled a yawn and then another one, and fell asleep partway through the narration. Lights dimmed on the singers and brightened over the centre of the stage where Subhadra tugged at the string of a cradle, rocking on her feet with the grace of a dancer and the beatific smile of a mother. Hema stole a glance at her friend. How much Shirley too must want a child. She seldom spoke about it. But it was good she hadn't let it colour her life. Little Abhimanyu played with bows and swords, and grew up to be a courageous warrior like his father. The great battle began. Drums beat and horses neighed offstage. The Kauravas laughed as they schemed. They were bound to win this round, since Arjuna, the only one who knew how to beat a chakravyuha, was engaged on a far-off warfront. In the Pandava camp, young Abhimanyu approached his worried uncles and explained how, when he was still in the womb, he had heard his father describe to his mother the technique of breaking into a chakravyuha. He didn't know how to exit, however, for his mother had dozed off at that point, but he was willing to improvise, he said. War music picked up again. Abhimanyu fought his way through concentric circles of soldiers, piercing, beheading and proceeding into the heart of the formation. Now a dozen warriors danced and spun around him with great ferocity. They were older and more experienced, perhaps three times the boy's age. They attacked him in unison. Abhimanyu fought, faltered, and eventually fell to the ground. The music quietened. Subhadra, with grey-streaked hair and vacant eyes, appeared in the middle of the stage tugging at the string of the cradle. Slowly the lights went out.

Hema and Shirley were quiet on the drive back. The car wove its way through the shadows of Connaught Place. The play was so sad. Hema wished they hadn't gone.

HEMA PUT HER HAND on Mr Clarke's arm. 'Mr Clarke?' The striped throw had slipped to his feet. She gathered and folded it, then walked over to the console and turned off the radio.

'You're back, dear.' His voice was a bit hoarse after the nap, and he cleared his throat. 'Did you find everything?'

'Yes, except skimmed milk, so I bought semi-skimmed.' She piled the throw on the sofa's back.

Mr Clarke felt the dial of his watch with his index finger. 'Shall we have lunch? I was thinking sautéed onion and chicken.'

'I bought some naan today,' she told him as they walked to the kitchen. 'We can try it, if you like.'

Hema sliced a large onion. Through teary eyes, she watched Mr Clarke pull up his sleeves, turn on the stove, remove the pan from its hook, place it neatly on the hob, and reach for the decanter of oil next to the stove. At times she felt he could see just as well as anyone, that his vision was not as blurred or poor as he claimed. Some weeks ago he had spotted a spider in the corner of a wall, and when she asked, 'How could you see it, Mr Clarke?' he went into a lengthy description of his boyhood hobby of hunting and collecting spiders. She didn't mention the incident to Sanjay, for he would have immediately questioned Mr Clarke's integrity and whether she should continue working for him. Instead, she wrote to Shirley.

'Have you ever been to London, my dear?' he asked now.

'We passed through the city when we landed in England, but we haven't gone back since.'

'You should go for a weekend. It's a blighted city, but worth a visit.' He had spent Christmas and New Year's with his niece Lisa and her family in London. There was a picture of him and Lisa's girls on the fridge, the three in matching red sweaters. 'Did I tell you, dear, I forgot to pack my medicines when I went.' The oil began to sizzle and Hema slid the onions into the pan. He gave them a stir with a wooden spoon. 'Lisa had to call up my doctors and get prescriptions faxed. It was such a nuisance. I was so annoyed with myself, though Lisa said it was all right.'

'It could happen to anyone, I guess.' Hema rinsed the chopping board and knife.

'Sometimes I feel I'm not fit to live alone, that perhaps I should consider a care home ... But I like living here in my own house. I have my routine, and you come in every other day, we talk, read. I'm already looking forward to our walks when summer comes.'

Hema turned on the oven, and while it warmed, she buttered the naans. She too liked coming over to Mr Clarke's, reading to him and listening to the stories of his life. It was her only real engagement with the outside world, and though Mr Clarke wasn't really a friend, he didn't behave like an employer either, and she enjoyed the ease and rapport they had developed. Now sometimes she would fold her legs on the sofa, because reading, she felt, was not meant to be done with feet planted on the ground. It was an act of leisure, of forgetting the self. This job at Mr Clarke's had also become her means of experiencing and interacting with England, an opportunity to see English life at close hand. Sweaters were called jumpers; Mr Clarke drank more tea than an average Indian; Radio 3 played classical music at all hours. Only the chores bothered her, like the grocery shopping this morning. They were a waste of time – time that she could better spend at her desk writing. *But that's what the paycheque is for,* Shirley wrote, *to justify the mundane tasks. Hema, don't worry about Mr Clarke and his 'integrity'. I don't think it really matters whether he's blind or not. It can't be easy living alone, especially in old age. I'm sure he looks forward to the hour when you walk in through the door. Sometimes I worry for Francis and myself, what will happen when one of us passes away. It makes me wonder if that's the real reason people want children.*

Mr Clarke pulled down his sleeves and picked up the knife and fork. Hema ate with her hands, wrapping bites of naan around the chicken. 'It's quite good,' she said, surprised that the only seasoning he had used was salt and pepper.

'Anna didn't enjoy working in the kitchen, so I would cook. She liked to travel, go on adventures.' He bit into the naan as though it were a slice of toast. 'Did I ever tell you she came all the way to Germany to visit me? We hadn't seen each other in three years. The warden agreed to let me slip off on the way to the fields. He was a kind man, though you couldn't guess that from looking at his face.' He laughed. 'Anna and I spent a whole day and night together at an inn. It was a beautiful day, the only one in those five years.'

'Weren't the people at the inn suspicious of you two?'

'Anna knew passable German, her grandmother on her mother's side was Austrian, so we were okay. Do you think naan's healthier than bread, dear? It tastes better.'

They finished lunch and cleared the table. Hema turned on the kettle, while Mr Clarke padded back and forth in the living room for his after-meal exercise. Shirley had stopped her evening walk. *I can't go to the park any more, Hema. It's full of kids and young mothers with babies. I fear one of these days I might pick up a child and run home. Something tells me I'm capable of it, and it scares me.* Hema poured hot water into the mugs and stirred in milk and sugar.

They read 'Access to the Children'. It was raining dismally in thin, long drops. Mr Clarke had the striped throw all the way up to his shoulders. The days were still terribly short, and soon afternoon would fold into night.

'SHOULD WE GET MUTTON patties along with orange juice?' Shirley said. She looked somewhat changed. Her heart-shaped face seemed fuller and her tanned skin had acquired a sheen.

'Sure,' Hema said and the waiter noted the order in his little pad.

'Nice cardigan,' Shirley said.

'Thanks. I knit it two years ago.' It was a sleeveless green vest with wooden buttons.

'Really? I couldn't guess. It's lovely.'

'Thanks. So tell me, how have you been?' They were seeing each other after three months, though they spoke regularly over the phone. Shirley had been busy with a textbook she was editing, but this morning she called and asked Hema to meet her at United Coffee House. They took a corner table. It was early evening; the restaurant was fairly full.

'I'm good,' Shirley said. 'I'm pregnant.'

Hema's hand flew to her mouth. She got up and hugged Shirley. 'That's such good news.'

'I'm sorry I kept it from you, and sorry I didn't see you all this while.' She looked up into Hema's face. 'I just wanted to be sure, you know? Francis and I have been cheated before.'

'I understand.' She sat down. 'How far along are you?'

'Five months.'

'You are glowing, Shirley. You look beautiful.'

The waiter brought the patties and juice. Shirley put mint chutney on her plate and quickly ate a couple of patties. 'I hope I don't become hideously fat, but I feel hungry all the time. We've had to hire a full-time cook.'

'That's good. You should eat and rest.'

'The doctor says the same, at least about resting. We've been concerned about my blood pressure. It's on the higher side.' She sipped the juice and tried to brighten up. 'You know, the baby kicked last week. It was such a wonderful and strange feeling. Like there was a little fish bobbing inside me.'

That winter Hema taught Shirley how to knit. They bought butter-yellow wool for Shirley and size-ten needles, and Hema decided on a lilac nightgown for Priya. Shirley came over once a week, and they sat on the balcony with their knitting and enjoyed the sun and talked. Now and then they took a break to eat oranges or peanuts. 'It feels like I'm in one of your stories,' Shirley would say. She had been reading Hema's work, taking home a new story every time. And as they sat on the balcony discussing them, Hema felt the stories gained a life of their own and from black-and-white turned into colour. Shirley encouraged her to send some to magazines. Their knitting grew by several inches every session. They designed press-studs on each shoulder for the baby's sweater so that it would be easy to put its head through. Sometimes Shirley tried to knit without looking at the needles, like Hema, and would drop a stitch. 'Oh fix this, Hema, please,' she would say then, pressing the needles into her hands.

To Hema's surprise, one of the magazines accepted her story. It sent two complimentary copies of the issue. In the evening Sanjay brought home rasgullas to celebrate the occasion. He hadn't read any of Hema's stories. He didn't read this one either. But he beamed at her name in the contents, then opened to her story and riffled through it as though to check how many pages it occupied. He was an accountant at an insurance firm, numbers made more sense to him than words. Still, as they sat in the living room after dinner, watching news and eating the rasgullas, Hema was happy. For the first time she thought perhaps she could put a collection together. She presented Shirley a copy of the magazine.

THE RAIN TURNED INTO a snow shower that bent and blew with the wind. Hema gripped the umbrella and pressed on. Across the road at The Bellevue, people sat at the bar chatting, their backs to the window, a fire flickering in the grate. Hema considered going in and ordering a cup of tea. If only she had a friend. She dug into her purse for her cap as she walked on. Shirley hadn't written this month, and Hema wondered if their friendship would fade eventually. Those evenings of leisure and long chats were certainly gone, never to return.

Snowflakes turned to water as they touched the pavement. It had been spring-like when she had left the house after lunch, but within an hour clouds had sealed off the sky, clouds as grey as those in the story she was working on this morning. She pictured the protagonist getting off the bus at Connaught Place, hair shabby, sari mud-splattered, asking a man the way to the Bata store. She saw her working her way to Connaught Circle while people waited under the eaves for the monsoon shower to let up. The second half of the story had unfolded in her head on the trek to and back from the post office. She liked the freedom of stepping out of the house whenever she wished, something she couldn't do in Delhi where she had to report her comings and goings to her mother-in-law. Sanjay had bought a second-hand car, and she too intended to get her driver's licence. She wrote to Shirley last night, sharing the news, and only adding in the final line that she hoped very much to hear from her soon. She passed the umbrella to her left hand and buried her right hand in a pocket. Ahead, two boys in red and blue jackets relieved the dull scenery. She had lost contact with her childhood friends after marriage. The distance and the responsibility of a new life had made staying in touch difficult. Her cousin Meera was in Delhi and Hema would visit her in her house adjoining the factory, and though they had never been close, their daughters played well together. Hema tried becoming friends with Sanjay's friends' wives, inviting them over for tea, going to sari shops with them, but she realized that there was no real basis for her friendship with these women like there was later with Shirley. She cherished how Shirley belonged just to her and she didn't have to share her with her husband or daughter. Matthew from next door was walking up the pavement, thick boots, collar up. He waved at her, she said hello, and they passed each other. The neighbourhood was silent. Snow drifted down, powdering trees and rooftops. The street lamps looked gaunt. She missed Delhi, the heat, the bustle, and the familiarity of it all. She scrubbed her feet on the doormat, took out the key and let herself in.

THROUGH THE SCREEN DOOR, the house appeared dark. When Hema rang the bell, a light came on and a man, she assumed Francis, approached the door. Francis was tall, had a heavy moustache. He sat her in the living room and went to call

Shirley. The living room walls were bland. There was a dining table in one corner and a TV stood in front of the sofa set. On a small altar were pictures of Christ and Mother Mary. Somehow it didn't look like a house that could be Shirley's.

Shirley emerged from the bedroom, walking slowly. Her eyes were puffy. She wore a printed kaftan. Hema held out her hand and Shirley took it and sat down beside her. She gave a wan smile. 'Thank you for coming.'

'Of course. How are you?'

'Not good.' Her hair was unwashed and hung limply. She tucked it behind her ears.

Francis brought Hema water. He caressed Shirley's arm and said, 'Do you want anything?'

Shirley shook her head. 'You know, it was a boy,' she said to Hema.

After that evening Hema visited Shirley every week, bringing her movies, magazines, or books from the library, though they just piled up on the dresser untouched.

'Did you go out anywhere?' She placed a copy of R.K. Narayan's *My Days* on the dresser and returned last week's books to her bag. Dust coated the furniture and the bed looked like it hadn't been made in days. An overflowing ashtray lay on Francis's side. Hema opened the windows. The curtains billowed and a light breeze sailed in. Shirley curled up and turned towards the cupboards. She wore the same printed kaftan.

'Let's go to India Gate,' Hema said.

'Why?'

'Because it's a nice evening to go out.'

Shirley resisted, but having no more strength, it seemed, finally gave in.

They walked on the lawn, sandals in hand, and watched the sky grow dark and the street lamps come on lighting up India Gate. The grass was moist. Families were picnicking and children played with balloons and Frisbees. Hema and Shirley strolled to the far end of the lawn and back. A madari was making his two monkeys perform to the beat of a little drum. Hema and Shirley joined the small crowd of onlookers. 'See what a respectable man comes to after marriage,' the madari said. He beat the drum and the male monkey prostrated in front of his wife who wore a red-and-gold skirt. 'She's angry and won't go home with him.' He beat the drum again, and the monkey rolled in the grass, stood up and attempted to kiss the wife. The crowd laughed. Shirley smiled. They bought chana jor garam and went to sit at a bench. The rai jamun trees cast long shadows on the lawn.

Shirley ate slowly, one roasted chickpea at a time. 'Why did this happen to me, Hema? What have I done to deserve it?'

'You haven't done anything, Shirley. Some things just belie all explanation.'

'Francis says we should adopt, but I'm not sure. We had a big fight. He says he's tired of me.'

'I'm sure he didn't mean it. This can't be easy for him either.'

'All I know is that he cannot feel the loss the way I do. No one can.' She looked at Hema. 'What if I don't have it in me to love an adopted child?'

'Why would you think that? You are such a giving person, Shirley, that I can't imagine you not loving a child, your own or adopted.'

'You really believe that?'

Hema nodded.

They finished the chickpeas and started to pace again. The grass felt cool and soft under their feet.

'Do you think Francis and I will ever be happy again?'

'Of course you will be. This will pass. You'll see.'

'It's good to come out. We should do it more often.'

'Yes,' Hema said. She didn't want to give her the news today. Next week, she thought.

They slipped on their sandals and walked back to the car.

'I'll drive,' she said, and Shirley passed her the keys.

10 BELA ROAD

I REMOVE THE MEASURING TAPE from around my neck and put it in the drawer along with the shears and chalk. If Masterji comes on time, we can start with these salwar suits tomorrow. I fold the cut fabric, the back, the front, and the sleeves and put them away too. Cherry is lying by the bed with a scrap of yellow chiffon between her teeth. She's probably hungry or bored or both. I pick up the jigsaw box and turn off the fan and she follows me out.

Ram Rattan hasn't rolled up the chick blinds, and the veranda is cool and dark. I place the box on the table where the pieces I have assembled so far wait for me. I stop to appraise the progress. It's like a moth-eaten view of the Tower Bridge, with gaping holes in the scene. The bridge itself and the towers are missing, but I have the buildings in the background on the bank. They have been easy to do, owing to the varied colours, the old ones with brown brick façades and the new ones that glint blue and green in the evening light. 'Yes, Cherry?' She's barking. She's prodding the bamboo chicks with her head to find the gap. I tug at the rope to raise them. Light rolls in and climbs up the veranda walls. I secure the rope around a pillar. Mom is watering the pomegranate tree, drops slipping off the leaves to form a puddle at the bottom. Cherry stands at the lip of the veranda and wags her tail. The henna streaks in Mom's hair shine copper. She waters the shaggy roses and the bed of canna lilies. Sparrows are chirping on the garden wall amongst the bougainvillea.

I sit on the sofa and sift through the pieces in the box. There are still so many of them. I find a lavender corner piece with two smooth edges and keep it aside on the table to use when it's time to patch the sky and the reflecting waters of the Thames. Cherry splays herself on the floor and rests her chin on my slipper. I stroke her with my toes. Mom has moved to the far side of the garden to water the mulberries. A bus trundles by on Shahdara Bridge, making the sparrows jump and scatter. The bridge passes just outside the house, but its fat, ugly pillars screen us from the main road, which is always busy. Three sparrows return to the bougainvillea. I riffle some more and spy what may be the top storey of the building on the right. I try it and it interlocks perfectly.

Ram Rattan brings cold coffee, tea and a couple of Marie biscuits and sets down the tray. 'Where's your mother?' he says in his sullen voice and goes out to the garden. The air smells muddy and moist. Cherry lifts her head and winks at the biscuits. I slide one off the tray and she catches it in her mouth. I sift through the box again, letting the pieces run through my fingers. I should start with the towers, don't think it can be put off any longer. I search for beige pieces. I find one, and one more. I chance upon a crenelated balcony. Cherry looks like a large rat, the way she is nibbling at the biscuit.

Mom takes off her slippers before stepping on to the veranda. She sits in the chair and reaches down to rub Cherry. 'Bhardwaj called,' she says.

'When?'

'An hour ago. He's bringing a buyer tomorrow. It's two brothers. They have a steel business. He says they are interested and want to see the house.' Cherry rolls on to her back, presenting Mom the length of her belly, eyes shut with pleasure.

'Did he say how much they are offering?'

'I asked twice, but he said we'll discuss that when we meet. Enough, Cherry. Come on. Good girl.' She picks up her tea and I sip at the coffee. I find a purple piece that could be one of the cruise boats on the Thames. 'Leave it alone,' Mom says. I was scratching behind my ear with the piece. I drove to Chandni Chowk this morning to buy chiffons, georgettes and laces for Simi's order, and then stood at the dyer's while he coloured and dried the fabrics. The air conditioner didn't work on the way back and I was soaked in sweat even before I reached Kashmere Gate. That could be when I got the sunburn, or perhaps it was at the dyer's. Anyway, the margin's going to be double since I sourced the fabrics myself. We should have the money from the suits next week, and the fixed deposit is maturing soon too. Hopefully we'll be okay for a while. Alcohol is getting expensive, so is meat. Sometimes Mom quips we should become vegetarians. The rent from the grocer's shop cancels out with what we buy from him every month. We can increase the rent by 10 per cent when the lease renews at the end of the year, but let's see, maybe the house will sell before then. I find two pieces of the golden steeple, tabs and blanks already linked.

Colour is seeping out of the sky and it's turned pale and peach. The heat is settling down. The sparrows have flown home. Bells are ringing at the Swaminarayan Temple and will continue for the next twenty minutes. Dad used to hate their incessant jangling, especially when he was bedridden and had to endure it every morning and evening. He had learned to complain effectively just using the corner of his mouth. A horn wails from the bridge, displacing the sound of the bells for a moment. Mom stretches her legs and Cherry creeps under. Maybe someone somewhere is doing a jigsaw of Shahdara Bridge with Mom, Cherry and me showing through its fat, ugly pillars.

I get up and switch on the lights. The pieces have become indistinct blotches of colour, and it is hurting my eyes to concentrate. The light is sallow. It always is in our house.

Ram Rattan passes by with a pile of ironed clothes to put in my room. I cross my legs on the sofa. My thighs are getting bulky. I should start going for a morning walk. Mom gets up, retrieves her slippers and goes to her room. Cherry is snoring. Outside, the sky is as lavender as the one over the Thames. It's beautiful how the summer sky segues from one colour to the next, and one can spend a whole evening just sitting here and looking out. In winter night arrives all too quickly. Ram Rattan emerges from the room, letting the screen door clap loudly behind him. I ask him to bring a table lamp from the drawing room. He grumbles under his breath. This present bout of surliness owes to the fact that Mom has ordered him to wear a shower cap in the kitchen. He places the lamp on the side table and jams the plug into the wall. Poor Ram Rattan. He does look funny in the cap, but we can't have his hair in our food, can we? 'Cherry, come. Dinner,' he says. Cherry opens her eyes, stretches and trots off after him to the kitchen.

The light is better now. I have a grey spire with the golden steeple on the top and a balcony complete with windows. The pieces are starting to link. Mom has turned on the tube light in her room, and I can see her through the wire mesh sitting on her bed, turning the pages of the paper. It will take us time getting used to living in a two-bedroom apartment in Gurgaon. I'm afraid it will be like living in a box, and like a rat one will always be trying to climb out. Here we have so much space. The garden looks placid, lit only by the lamps on the bridge. The mulberries have receded into the shadows. In Gurgaon, Mom will have to make do with a few pots on the balcony. But at least we won't have to worry about our finances all the time. At the first meeting, when Bhardwaj said we could expect thirty crore rupees or more, Mom's jaw dropped. Here we were, sitting on a gold mine yet barely making ends meet. Bhardwaj smirked and slurped at his tea. It's a large house, of course, that too in Civil Lines, but we never imagined actually selling it. Dad was too unwell to realize he was signing over his share of the business to his brother. Thankfully the house was in my name. Grandpa had bought it in the early fifties from a Muslim family that moved to Hyderabad after Partition. Grandpa loved its mix of Indian and English sensibilities – the long veranda with the two octagonal rooms on either end looking on to the garden, the high roshandans, the pantry alongside the kitchen – so he decided to keep the house as it was. I wish we could continue living here, but there's little point in being sentimental. We are already making lists of things we are going to buy: a big TV, new wardrobes, Mom wants a microwave and griller, we need a new car. We are thinking a Honda City. The Maruti is so old and battered, it's embarrassing driving around in it. Dad bought it nearly twenty years ago, after our sports equipment company received a contract for the Asian Games of '82.

Mom is clipping something from the paper, could be the three-cheese lasagna recipe she was talking about. For a while she ran a takeout restaurant from the back of the house where we have my workshop now, between Ram Rattan's quarters and the grocer's store. She called it 'Mrs Singh's Kitchen' and hired Ram Rattan's son to deliver the orders on his cycle. Everyone loves Mom's cooking. Her saag meat, chicken hara pyaz, kathi rolls and toffee pudding are popular in our circle. The toffee pudding is really nice and sticky. It's a nice sort of stickiness. My mouth's watering. The orders kept us busy the whole day, the phone rang every five minutes. It turned out to be more than Mom could handle. People started to complain that the food arrived too late, too cold. Mom doesn't take criticism very well. She closed down the restaurant. I think she still has the menus somewhere in her cupboard.

I didn't realize that the temple bells had stopped ringing. Ram Rattan is listening to the radio in the kitchen, and Cherry, it seems, is pushing her dinner bowl across the floor. I sit back to regard the twenty-odd miscellaneous beige pieces lined on the table. One with a crenelated moulding jumps out at me. I move it below the balcony and it fits. I review the image on the box. There ought to be windows below here. This piece maybe, and this one. Ah, I almost have two storeys of the left tower. The doorbell rings. Cherry comes running from inside the house and shoots out to the garden and the gate beyond. Ram Rattan ambles after her, digging in his ear with a matchstick. I patch together the arch where the tower meets the bridge to let the traffic through. I move the arch and the balcony along with the lower storey to their probable places on the table. The view still looks moth-eaten, but the gaps are filling up.

Simi appears on the veranda panting, with Ram Rattan restraining Cherry by the collar while she tries to paw towards Simi. 'Don't let go of her,' Simi warns.

'She likes you,' I say. 'See how she's wagging her tail.'

'No, please.' Simi shakes her head, making her diamond earrings wiggle. She's wearing a pastel green lakhnavi, with the dupatta wrapped like a shawl. 'I just stopped to check on my suits.' She looks my way, and like always, her squint disconcerts me.

'I'm going to put them into production tomorrow.' I arrange the remaining beige pieces in a line.

'Satsriakal.' Mom emerges from her room. She hugs Simi. 'Congratulations on your sister-in-law's engagement.'

'Thank you, Auntie. We are going to the boy's for a dinner party just now. Param and my sister-in-law are in the car outside.'

Cherry barks. She tries to sink her teeth into Ram Rattan's hand, and he flicks her ear.

'Ram Rattan, no,' Mom says. The house is a bit livelier with all of us on the veranda and Simi's lovely earrings. Mom and I should go out for dinner sometime, maybe we could go to Chor Bizarre. They always play nice old Bollywood songs.

'Where does the boy's family live?' Mom asks.

'Punjabi Bagh. They are an old Delhi family. Sound, good people, Auntie.'

'That's nice. Don't forget you have to find a boy for your friend too.'

Simi smiles. It is hard to say whether she's looking at Mom or me. The squint came a few years after the marriage, and I'm not sure if she's really happy.

'Do you want to quickly see the fabrics?' I say.

She nods, swaying her earrings. We go to my room and Mom takes Cherry to hers.

Simi sits on the bed. 'I haven't been to your room in a long time.' She looks around. 'But nothing really changes in this house, does it? You still have the same watercolour paintings on the wall and the picture with your dad. I think I even remember this embroidered bedcover.'

I smile. We used to sit together on the school bus. Now she has a fifteen-year-old son whom she drops at and collects from the same stop. I show her the fabrics. She likes the lilac georgette and approves of the yellow chiffon too. 'The blue is similar to what I'm wearing today. I was thinking more aqua.'

'Sure. We can do that.' She usually doesn't like Masterji's stitching and places an order only when she needs something urgently.

A horn blares outside, two-and-a-half toots. 'That's Param! I'll go. Just please get everything done by next week.' She rushes out. 'Bye, Auntie.' She waves across the veranda at Mom and clatters off.

I keep the fabrics in the cupboard, turn off the light and return to the jigsaw. Mom is on the phone in her room, cradling the base in her lap. Cherry is lying by the bed. I cross my legs on the sofa and focus on the jigsaw. From the miscellaneous row, I move a portion of a window to the lower storey of the left tower. It interlocks. I check for the adjoining pieces. Simi's perfume lingers in the air.

'Dinner is ready,' Ram Rattan says.

Mom's still on the phone. I close the jigsaw box and pass it to him to keep in my room.

The table is laid. There's fresh naan in the roti basket. Cherry ambles in and settles down next to my chair. Ram Rattan pours water from the jug. Everything replicates in the long mirror on the opposite wall. The mirror is freckled in one corner. It almost looks stained. The white-and-red chandelier overhead has grown lacklustre and gives off a milky light. Simi is right. Nothing ever changes in this house. I can remember forever eating from these plates with a rose border. This one is chipped at the edge. I feel its roughness with my thumb. Atul found all this charming. It lends the place character, he observed. He liked these old, hand-painted runners too, and when Mom said she had got them done by a Kashmiri from Chandni Chowk, he scribbled a note in his pad. He wanted to write an article about the house and had come to us through Tejinder Auntie. He carried a backpack and wore sandals instead of shoes. He was handsome, though not good-looking. We asked him to stay for lunch. Mom cooked. The article featured in *The Brunch* as 'The Last Colonial Bungalow'. It opened with an impressive photograph of the façade, which Atul had shot from the bridge, adjusting the light so as to camouflage the peeling paint. In between paragraphs were pictures of the garden with the mulberries in bloom, the veranda with its white colonnade and cane furniture, the crossed swords on the drawing room wall, and Cherry curled up in one of the ornate chairs. Atul wrote that our house had a great sense of having been lived in. Mom wanted to frame the article and hang it in the drawing room, but I thought it would make us feel we lived in a museum. Maybe we can hang it in the new apartment. Right above our beds. I laugh. Cherry looks at me. 'Nothing, Cherry.' I stroke her chin and she licks my hand. 'I'm just being pathetic.'

Mom takes her place at the head of the table. She lets out a sigh as she places the napkin in her lap.

'What happened?' I serve myself some keema and pass her the bowl. The naans are warm and fluffy.

'Kuku's wife hit him.'

I'm sure she had reason enough, but Mom is looking at me so I have to ask, 'Why?'

'They had an argument over his petrol expenses. He says his face is swollen. You know how thick her fingers are.'

Cherry is smacking her lips. Her nose is quivering. I wrap some keema in naan and give it to her. I hope Kuku Mama will lie low for a while and won't bring more proposals from widowers and divorced men.

'I've asked him to come stay with us for a few days.'

'Why?' He's going to eat all the meat in the freezer, ordering Ram Rattan to make shami kebabs and mutton curry and keema paranthas. In a week Ram Rattan will be threatening to leave.

'He always looks out for us, doesn't he? It was his idea we sell the house.'

I can only sigh. I hate the thought of him lounging on the veranda all day in his vest.

'It's good he'll be here tomorrow when Bhardwaj comes with the brothers.'

Ram Rattan clears the table and brings the chocolate cake Mom baked yesterday. The shower cap gives him a matronly air.

Cherry is clawing at my chair for a piece. Mom scolds her and she barks back in the same tone, making Mom laugh. She calls out to Ram Rattan to bring Cherry a biscuit.

The cake is rich and moist. I suggest serving some with tea tomorrow. Mom agrees. She cuts the remaining cake into slices. We decide on cream-and-cheese toasts and aloo medallions as well.

Mom and I watch the nine o'clock news. I pour her whisky and fix myself a gin with lemon juice and sugar. Mom flips channels during the ad break to catch up on her soap. She has to press the worn keys of the remote with both hands, and for a second it looks like she's shooting at the TV. I go sit by Cherry on the bed. The news was boring in any case. I sip at the gin. The glass looks pretty with sugar crystals on the rim. Cherry is lying with her head on Dad's pillow. I stroke her ear. It's warm and velvety and long. When she was little, her ears were so large compared to the rest of her that they swept the floor. Mom shoots at the TV to return to the news. Two years ago, she decided we should get Cherry mated and sell her babies. She figured that even at 7,000 per baby, we could make 35,000 a year. We had the vet calculate Cherry's ovulation cycle and paired her with three different beagles, three different times. It turned out Cherry is barren. There's a tick on the underside of her ear. I pluck it and carry it to the toilet. Mom's handwash has a refreshing orangey smell. I might sleep with Mom and Cherry today. I don't feel like sleeping alone. I return to the room to find Cherry scratching at the screen door. 'I'll take her,' I say, and Mom nods. Her glass is already half empty. She might have a second drink tonight.

Cherry scuttles to the garden with her nose to the ground. I turn on the tube light and walk to the gate to switch on the lamps over the gatepost. The neighbours must be out. Our Maruti stands alone under the bridge. Over at the Swaminarayan Temple, fruit and flower vendors sit in the glow of their gas lamps waiting for after-dinner customers. Ram Rattan's son pedals up, whistling a tune.

I pace outside the veranda while Cherry sniffs around the garden to pick a spot. She's considering the queen of night. The flagstones are still giving off heat, and the sky is a flaming purple, almost the colour of the bougainvillea that covers the wall. The night is calm though. The jigsaw pieces rest on the table, and on the bridge cars whizz up and down smoothly. Gurgaon is all concrete and business-like, too new to really have a sense of self. It wouldn't match our temperament. I sniff a lock of my hair. It smells sweet after the shampoo this morning. What if the house knows we are selling it? I look up, and the house looks back kind of sad. The cheap whitewash has given it an indigo pallor. I hope the brothers won't tear it down to make cramped, unappealing apartments, but that's been the fate of most old properties around here. The families moved outside Delhi, to Noida, Ghaziabad or Gurgaon. This is a beautiful house. It is meant to be lived in. I hope the brothers will allow us to visit once in a while and sit on the veranda with a cup of tea. Cherry is peeing on the mint, one leg raised. It is her favourite spot.

STEEL BROTHERS

IT WAS WARM INSIDE the car which smelt of jasmine, and on the CD player Farida Khanum sang an alap. Unaccompanied, she let her voice loose, made it meander. The road was packed, ruby tail lights as far as the eye could see, street lamps smudged by the smog that had settled over the city, the heater weaving its own patch at the edge of the windshield.

'Looks like it will be an hour before we reach home,' Roshan said. 'Let's stop at Joshaba.'

Kamal nodded his silver head.

Roshan honked, inched the car leftward, honked again, braked. The green arrow tick-tocked on the dashboard, matching tempo with the tabla, while traffic trickled by on either side. Kamal lowered the window and waved his arm, causing a Maruti to brake. The driver cursed. The brothers cursed back. They reached the far lane finally and turned left, leaving behind the clogged main road and its screeching horns. A letter box on the curb stood dusty red.

The traffic was lighter here, and the car rolled smoothly for the first time since the brothers had left the factory. Roshan rolled his shoulders, eased back in his seat. Khanum sang languorously, fuller throated than before, as though she too had a sudden sense of freedom. Roshan felt like pulling out a cigarette, but for a while now he had been sensing Kamal's distaste, so new and abrupt that it was puzzling, the way he swatted at the smoke or rolled down his window. On the pavement smoke curled up from the clay pot of a peanut seller, shops rushed by, a woman in a gaudy blue shawl, or was it a mannequin? Roshan glanced in the wing mirror. Men huddled around a bonfire, toasting palms.

'Did you give Mr Henry the new catalogue?' Roshan asked.

'I told Verma to put it in the car for him. I highlighted the round snack warmer so that Mr Henry would remember it.'

'Good. I think he'll order a small consignment to start with. In case he doesn't, remember to send him a few complimentary pieces with the next shipment.' Roshan had worked for months perfecting the snack warmer, improving remarkably on the Chinese sample it was modelled after, smoothening the joints, replacing the curved legs with straight ones for a modern look, instructing the operator on how to buff its edges to roundness, making the polishwala work until the snack warmer gleamed like a trophy. It was an expensive product with a 100 per cent margin. Mr Henry's visit could not have been better timed.

Roshan slowed down. He could see the grill jutting out of the tiny kebab shop, chicken strung on skewers, partially roasted, curled tight, glistening with marinade, and three men eating busily at a plastic table set on the pavement. He parallel parked in a tight spot, cut off the engine, but let Khanum sing.

'So, malai tikka?' Kamal said. 'One plate each?' He lowered the briefcase that he had been holding between his knees into the seat well and climbed out of the car. A cash payment had come in today for a batch of pet bowls for which only a handwritten bill had been drawn without logging it in the books, and the brothers were taking the money home to keep with their mother. Among her other talents, she could open a heavily stapled bundle by giving it an expert twist and pulling it apart at the same time. Of her two sons, Roshan was her favourite.

'Don't forget the chutney and onions.'

Kamal ducked at the window to nod. His silver hair – caused by sinusitis, according to the family homeopath – made him appear the elder of the two. He had large eyes, though they didn't betray much, and their mother's compressed lips. He snuck his hands into his coat pockets and padded off towards the shop.

Roshan lit a cigarette and turned up the volume. Khanum's laments filled the car, her voice husky, torn, like curdling milk, like a cloth ripped rather than cut. *'Mohabbat karne wale kum na honge / Teri mehfil mein lekin hum na honge.'* Roshan hummed along. An urchin, a boy in shorts despite the weather, hurried across the road with a steaming plate of biryani. He knocked at the window of a parked car, passed the plate in and scampered back, picking his way through the thin traffic. Kamal stood by the grill, watching the cook rotate the skewers. The cook fanned the coals and sparks erupted, a burst of fireflies. In the car ahead, two silhouettes shared a plate, almost forming a heart. Roshan exhaled smoke through his nostrils. He remembered the Black Label lying in the dicky. He took a long puff, smoking an inch of the cigarette, and climbed out of the car. Kamal was still at the grill, arms folded, always on the defence.

Roshan returned with the whisky, and with plastic cups and club soda that he had procured a few shops down. He poured two drinks, holding the cups against the street light, mauve rather than orange as it slanted in, ensuring the peg was neither smaller nor larger than what he had every evening.

He leaned and opened the passenger door, and Kamal slid into the seat, holding aloft plates of tikka piled with red onion rings. Kamal smiled, noticing the whisky. 'Where did this come from?' He passed Roshan a plate, and the brothers lifted the drinks from the holder. Carefully, they touched the brimming cups together. 'Cheers.' Not loquacious by nature, the brothers didn't say it, but they were toasting

Mr Henry's successful visit. They brought the brimming cups to their lips. The aroma of the tikkas saturated the air, a heady fragrance of flesh roasted patiently on charcoal. The tikkas were tender, coated with creamy marinade, instantly dissolving in the mouth. It had been a long but good day at the factory. After the welcome tea, they had taken Mr Henry, Procurement Manager, Beckman & Co., for a tour, stopping first at the original karkhana their father had built in the sixties, somewhat cavernous, smelling of grease, but busy, a giant cogwheel machine dominating the floor. They escorted him next to the new workshop that had a salmon brick façade and stood in the shade of a grand neem tree. This workshop was large, modern; the brothers had set it up three years ago after exports took off. Here they walked Mr Henry from station to station as Kamal explained the process of manufacturing a kadhai, showing him first how steel was rendered malleable in the electric furnace at 1100 °C, then conducting him towards the final step when handles would be fitted on to the buffed utensil. The kadhai, or balti dish as it was known in the US, was Beckman & Co.'s largest import, and Roshan had designed the tour around it. Now he walked with his hands clasped behind him, like the pigeons on the wide windowsills, while Kamal, who spoke better English, led. The silver hair gave Kamal a certain suaveness, a polish he hadn't possessed in his youth. One hand ensconced in his trouser pocket, he let Mr Henry know that the family had been in this line of business for three quarters of a century, with their father eschewing the traditional brass for the versatile stainless steel when he re-established the business in Delhi after Partition. At the deep-draw hydraulic press, they watched the operator mould a plate of steel into a wok as easily as though it were wax. Kamal was supposed to tell Mr Henry that the hydraulic press, imported from Germany, was one of its kind in India, but when he didn't, Roshan cleared his throat and hesitantly supplied the information himself.

Kamal blew his nose now, folded the napkin. 'Verma's taking the day off tomorrow, so we'll have to stop at the bank ourselves on the way to the factory.'

Roshan took a large sip of the whisky. He placed the cup back in the holder. 'I think Verma's sullen because I set him to clean the filing room. He was limping more than usual today.' Verma's limp tended to worsen and improve with his mood. Addressed as Verma Sahib even by the brothers, he was a retired public-sector bank manager who looked after the accounts for the business. Additionally, on days when the brothers had an argument, he was made to hobble between their offices with documents Kamal needed Roshan to sign or a sales query Roshan had for Kamal. He shared a desk with the clerk in the filing room, which had been the mother's bedroom when the family still resided in the factory. One morning, he limped into the office, lunch pail in hand, hair flattened by the helmet, to find the clerk using the company internet and watching porn. Verma cordially reported the incident to Kamal.

'Verma asked why we didn't bring Mr Henry to the filing room. He had spent three days sifting through old documents and ledgers. He thought we overdid the preparations.' Roshan had a coloured catalogue designed to showcase the inventory. A fresh coat of paint was considered for the office. He got every surface, switchboard and fan blade scrubbed thoroughly. Net curtains were ordered. The wives were sent to Gaffar Market to buy a bone china tea set and Danish cookies. 'I doubt Mr Henry noticed the new curtains, and we put them up in such a rush.' Kamal looked sidelong at his brother.

A lot would not be possible if we didn't have Beckman & Co.'s business, the new house, for example, the boys' education, Roshan would have replied, but his shoulders felt tense, his toes weary. He bunched a tikka with some onion and placed it in his mouth. The tikka was warm, so was the plate. He weighed the plate in his palm. Low-grade steel, lacklustre, easily dented, possibly from a factory in Wazirpur. He cleaned the yogurt-and-mint chutney with a plump finger and licked it. Outside, a car cruised by, one headlight out. The road lapsed once again into its mauve darkness. The tanpura struck a plaintive note. A pack of skinny dogs loped from car to car, sniffing at windows, hoping for a bone, a shred of meat.

'Mother was saying she wants to gift one lakh rupees at Radha Auntie's grandson's wedding.'

'One lakh!' Roshan said, eyes wide. A similar sum had already been spent on wedding clothes for the family and plane tickets to Amritsar. Only Roshan was staying back since a consignment was sailing out the same weekend. The final inspections done, the cartons on their way to the port in Bombay, Roshan planned to remain in bed on Sunday, smoke and sleep. In the evening he would drive to Dilip's guitar store for drinks, and later dine with him and Deepa in their apartment upstairs that could be accessed from the outside by a wrought-iron staircase. But now, Mother wanting to give away one lakh rupees threatened the equanimity of the weekend. She was part-owner of the business, holding a third of the share, and from time to time liked to make her weight felt.

'I told her it isn't like we have a money-minting machine, but she got angry.'

'I'll try and speak with her, let's see,' Roshan said.

'Anuj and Raghu's semester fees are due soon too.'

Roshan nodded. He contemplated the shimmering whisky. Apropos of his thoughts, Khanum sang '*Sari duniya ke ranj-o-gum dekar / Muskurane ki baat karte ho*'. The rupee was at a high of thirty-nine against the dollar, and while that was working out for exports, school fees for the University of North Dakota had become more expensive than the year before. The brothers just hoped that, equipped with an American education, their sons would one day manage the business even better than them. But for now, the two toiled alone to fulfil the needs and fancies of a family of eight. The stress of running the business had given Roshan his dark, aubergine-coloured lips, for he couldn't think without a cigarette, and Kamal his prematurely grey hair.

Roshan turned towards his brother and crossed one leg on the seat. He thought of extracting his feet from the flawlessly polished Florsheims but only wiggled his toes. 'Yaar,' he said, 'I was speaking with the broker yesterday and he suggested some bank stocks, said they could quadruple within a year. I think we should invest. It's been six years.'

Kamal crossed his arms, elbows pointy even through the coat.

On the pavement, the urchin wiped the plastic table for a scarfed, heavily bundled family of four. Joshaba hung behind powdery fog, the blue of its billboard grainy.

Roshan mopped up a tikka with the chutney. 'If you're still thinking about what Verma said, I don't believe he can really read palms. He couldn't have foreseen our loss in the stock market.'

'He did though, and quite accurately.' Kamal rotated the mirthless red stone on his finger. 'In any case, we should consider chopping down the neem.'

It was rather touching how he brought up the tree now and then. But the neem had stood in the compound for as long as Roshan could remember, offering shade in summer, staying green through winter. He felt the tree said something about the years the factory itself had accumulated, the life it had seen, the experience it had gained. At night, soaked in moonlight, it looked like it was made of stainless steel.

That slow afternoon, however, after the palm reading and just before Verma lurched out with helmet and pail, he leaned importantly on his short leg and said that, according to Vastu Shastra, the tree was in the wrong corner and in time would sap the brothers' relationship of all love and light (or something to that effect). Neither Roshan nor Kamal had repeated the words thereafter, for that would have been a touch sentimental. The brothers never hugged each other, there was never a reason to. When they wished one another 'Happy Birthday' every year, there was an awkwardness on both sides. In the family albums, there was no picture of just the two of them. Sipping the last of the whisky, Roshan wondered what would happen to the business if their relationship crumbled. The thought was many pronged. He felt like a smoke. The red-and-gold box lay in the small space behind the gear stick.

'Should we order some seekh kebab?' Kamal said. In the dark of the car, his nose shone pink. Sinusitis was a sign of repressed anger, Verma had said. Kneading the mounds of Kamal's palm, some cushiony, some flat, he observed Kamal was ambitious, hardworking, but he never got his due, to which Kamal nodded, lips compressed, chin dimpled. Verma was an old rat in a double-breasted coat, trying to claw a place for himself in the fast-changing world. In the lines in Roshan's palm, he read his ill luck at the stock market and ostensibly the Harshad Mehta scam that followed six months later, turning the brothers' colossal holdings to rubble.

The urchin was on the other side of the road, delivering a food packet. Roshan honked and signalled him over, then unscrewed the cap and refreshed their cups.

'Chotu, two plates mutton seekh kebab,' he said when the boy appeared at the window, 'two rumalis, and don't forget the chutney and onion.' He glanced at Kamal's pink nose. 'Some napkins as well,' he added.

The urchin nodded and scurried to the shop, stopping for a second to kick a scabby dog in the flanks and send it yelping into a dark alley. The night had grown chillier, tinged with more mauve, benumbed by the cold. Roshan rolled up the window.

'Tum hi socho zara kyun na rokein tumhein / Jaan jati hai jab uthke jate ho tum.' Khanum held the notes in her fist, reined them in, then let go with an unfurling of slender fingers. Every evening Roshan waited for the CD to come round to this ghazal, number six in line. He hummed along despite himself. Through the cold windshield, the tail lights of the next car appeared smeared. He had heard Farida Khanum for the first time at Dilip's guitar store, late one evening as the dim lights deepened in the mirror behind the counter. If there hadn't been a picture on the cover, he would have imagined Khanum to be like Deepa, sculpted cheekbones, a faint scent of guavas. His fingers tapped the steering, eyes shut. Khanum's voice seeped to the part of him that was an artist, an architect, a romantic. And he would have become all those things if he hadn't dropped out of school

to work at the karkhana after their father passed away. He had learned to compensate for his education by talking less, by ironing the creases of his trousers until they were razor sharp, by wearing shoes a size small to make his bulky feet look elegant. He wiggled his toes now, enjoying the cramped feeling, the pain from the ingrown toenails. Before bed, he ritually soaked his feet in warm water, smoked another cigarette. '*Yoon hi pehlu mein baithe raho...*' Khanum sang with leisure, slowing the world to a churn. Roshan reached for the cigarettes, then remembering, drew back his hand. He turned on the ignition and switched on the heater. The clock blinked 7.45. Another thirty minutes.

'Is that Ravi Sood?' He pointed to a white Mercedes across the road. A gold-ringed hand gleamed on the steering.

Kamal peered. 'He's sending his son to the US too. Same university as Anuj and Raghu.' He glanced at Roshan. The brothers exchanged a smile.

Roshan shook his head. He felt somewhat loosened by the whisky and his head wobbled more than he had intended it to. Kamal had been a good foot soldier and the brothers had come far together, but it had to be said, and he said it: 'No one's ridden the wave better than Sood.'

Sood flashed the dipper and beckoned to the urchin with his ringed fingers. The boy rushed towards the car, almost colliding with a scooter in his haste. Sood was once a mere clerk at the government-owned Steel Authority of India Limited. He would ride in an autorickshaw to the brothers' factory twice a month, a faux leather pouch, the sort cheap merchants carried, dangling from his wrist. No rings back then. He would go round behind the karkhana where scrap lay in a shapeless, thorny cloud. He would stuff the scrap into jute sacks, hunker down with a long needle to stitch the mouths, load the sacks into the waiting rickshaw, and take them to the steel market in Naraina. Today he owned an export–import company and three manufacturing units – one produced cutlery, another surgical instruments, and the third top-of-the-line chafing dishes – all in the seven years since the markets had opened up in 1991, freeing trade, pegging the rupee to the dollar. In the beginning, with the new money, Sood emulated the brothers, getting his trousers and suits stitched at Jagdish Tailors in Connaught Place, buying a royal blue Maruti 1000 (the brothers owned a white one), transferring his son to the school Raghu and Anuj went to. Now, of course, he had surpassed them in wealth. Now if he visited the factory, he sat in the office with the brothers, instead of behind the karkhana. He was the one who gave them the name 'Steel Brothers', or at least the brothers liked to credit him for it.

The urchin wore a woollen cap on his shorn head when he showed up with their order. A warm fragrance of minced meat and chillies plumed from the kebabs. 'What took you so long?' Roshan said, his mouth watering. 'Now bring the bill in ten minutes.'

The car filled with the sound of the brothers eating, for a while drowning Khanum out. The kebabs were cinnamon-coloured, licked with oil, dripping with juices. In between bites, the brothers doused the onion rings in chutney and chomped them intently.

Kamal blew his nose, snivelled, wiped his nostrils. 'I booked a table for four at House of Ming tomorrow.' He folded the napkin.

'Chinese?'

'Chinese. At the Taj.' Kamal's wife was convent educated; marriage had refined his tastes. 'Would you and bhabhi like to join? I could change the booking.'

Roshan shook his head. In any case, he preferred the narrow, dimly lit Fujian tucked away in Connaught Place, where the staff knew him and the hot and sour soup was excellent – a dash of soya sauce, just the right amount of vinegar. He would have liked, though, to sit down for a drink with Mr Henry, and attaining a certain volubility, recount the story of how he found Beckman & Co.'s contact. A family relation, who exported rice to the Middle East, happened to tell him that people were using the internet to expand their businesses. The handiness of the idea, its feasibility, appealed to Roshan, and he had the computer moved to his room. Every night after he had soaked his feet, he searched Yahoo and Altavista for importers, sent out introductory emails, and noted down addresses to dispatch samples to the next day. Finally, at around 12 o'clock, he squeezed two drops of Cineraria into his dry eyes, savoured its brief burning sensation, and retired to bed. It was a few days before Dussehra, a year had passed, at least a thousand emails had been sent out, when he stumbled across Beckman & Co.'s listing that described it as a manufacturer of premium melamine products and a supplier of world-class food service equipment. He would tell Mr Henry he still remembered spotting in the attached picture of the New York showroom, on the far side of the second shelf, a stainless-steel round roasting tray with rack. Roshan had three international buyers today, but Beckman was still his biggest find. At this point, he would shake Mr Henry's absurdly large hand. With his little finger, Roshan pried some meat from between his molars. 'What time are you meeting Mr Henry for dinner?' he asked, mouth tasting faintly of cloves.

'Seema's taking his wife to Janpath in the afternoon, so I booked the table for eight.'

'Don't be late.'

'Of course not.'

Roshan smiled, easy from the alcohol. But this morning, when Kamal had got them late for the factory again and the two found themselves at a thirty-degree slant in the jam on Shadipur flyover, Roshan had lost his temper, face red, the many moles ready to pop like mustard seeds. Kamal stayed quiet, neither arguing nor apologizing. Arms folded, he looked out of the windshield. They arrived at the factory well after ten to find the curtainwala waiting with the new curtains. The rest of the morning the brothers avoided each other, communicating only through Verma. The curtains were barely up, the office boy still picking wayward threads and hooks off the floor, when the family driver, who along with a car had been put at Mr Henry's service, drove him through the large rust-coloured factory gate.

'Let Mr Henry and his wife order whatever they like, drinks, duck, dessert,' Roshan said. 'Don't hold back.'

Kamal snivelled.

Outside, the fog had eaten parts of the road, shuttering shops before they actually closed down. Sood's car had left, and in its place stood a banana cart shawled in fog. The tabla percussed, Khanum's voice bloomed, making up for the lack of the moon. The brothers unfurled their rumalis on their plates, lay the last seekhs on them, layered them with onion rings, dribbled the green chutney along their lengths, and then rolled the rumalis tight as cigars. It was oddly reassuring, this harmony of their movements. Almost in unison, they bit through the soft, handkerchief-thin rumalis, into the crunchy onion, past the chutney to reach the succulent kebabs. Kamal nodded his approval of the roll to Roshan. Roshan nodded back. The tax accountant had recently told Roshan that Kamal had borrowed money from the joint business to start up an electrical cable trade. Verma hadn't uttered a word, though he must have known. The young tax accountant suggested that Roshan also look after his own interests. The brothers had spent five years in building the new house, lovingly and painstakingly supervising each stone laid, every arch constructed. Together they selected doorknobs, bath fittings, stone grilles for the balconies. Then Roshan let Kamal pick the largest room, the one with five spacious closets and a grand sunk marble bath. To this day, Roshan's wife was upset about the closets. He hadn't shared with anyone yet the tax accountant's revelation. Kamal bent his silver head and looked into the seat well. 'Under the seat,' Roshan said. Kamal bent further, drew out the briefcase and clamped it between his knees. The brothers returned to the rolls.

The urchin knocked on the window. He passed toothpicks and saunf on a plate. 'A sahib in a white Mercedes paid your bill.'

Roshan shared the information along with the toothpicks and saunf with Kamal. He fished out his wallet and tipped the boy.

Roshan turned on the headlights and eased the car on to the foggy road. *'Shukriya, shukriya,'* Khanum breathed as the last recording came to an end and the audience broke into applause. The CD gave a few guttural clicks and spun to begin again. Roshan didn't play the CD in the morning. In the morning, the brothers drove in silence.

WEEKEND IN LANDOUR

ABHAY LINED HIS WALLET, Blackberry and Marlboros on the desk and went to the window.

Outside there was a lawn, and beyond that the valley from which tall trees grew, their branches like drooping moustaches. Far off, the mountains were dotted with huts, and mist drifted over the peaks.

The porter set down the luggage. 'Anything else you need, sir?'

'No, just take this one next door to madam's room.' Abhay pointed to Megha's striped overnight bag. He drew a fifty from his wallet.

The porter smiled. Deep creases showed on his face, even though he was not an old man. He took the money, picked up the bag, salaamed and left.

Abhay sat down in the chair and lit a cigarette. He took a puff, crossed one leg over the other. A glass, a water jug, and an orange flower in a vase stood on the desk. A checked blanket lay at the foot of the bed. He got up and sniffed it. It smelled woolly but clean. There was no phone in the room, which meant no room service. Two upturned lamps shaped like tulips grew out of the wall on either side of the bed. All the big hotels in Mussoorie were booked when he had called the day before. It was July, but the monsoons had not arrived yet and the severe heat of the plains had driven people to hill stations at the foot of the Himalayas. Megha had called him and talked about how tired she was of Delhi, the heat, the pollution, the grit that got into her sandals when she walked in the streets, and he had listened, idling through some construction drawings. 'It would be nice to get away for a few days,' she said. 'Want to go to Mussoorie?' he asked, laughing.

They had met two years ago at a photography exhibition, while Megha waited to interview the artist and Abhay stood in a corner sipping wine. Since then, they had got together a handful of times for coffee. He had been mildly attracted to her at first. She had long legs, wore her hair in a high ponytail, and worked as the arts editor of a magazine. She had a thick mole on the tip of her chin which he didn't like, but in any case things never got romantic between them. And so it surprised him when she replied, 'Hmm ... Why not? We can go the day after tomorrow.' Then she added, 'Book two rooms, okay?' 'Sure. Of course,' he said. He searched the internet and finally found this cottage in Landour, a few kilometres above Mussoorie. He wondered now if she intended him to pay for her room.

He crushed the cigarette in the ashtray and reached for his phone. There were a few messages but none from Kavya. He hadn't called her in many days, and she hadn't contacted him either. He picked up the room key, and on the way out checked the phone again. Nothing. 'Good,' he said.

The pink-and-green carpet of the room covered the corridor as well, its design smudged out by years of wear. Abhay knocked at Megha's door.

'Come in,' she called.

He found her sitting on the bed, legs stretched and crossed at the ankles.

'Want to have lunch?' he asked. 'There's a dining room downstairs. We can try it out.'

She got up from the bed, picked up her cardigan from where it hung on the back of the chair and draped it over her shoulders. 'Let's go.'

They asked for lunch to be served on the lawn, where they sat now under a wide umbrella. The cottage was colonial, with a sloping green roof and a faded cream façade. A weathered stone staircase led up to it from the road. They could see a part of the road from where they sat, before it curved and disappeared round the bend.

'Are those pine trees?' Abhay said, pointing to the valley.

'Could be deodars.'

Abhay nodded. He chewed on the inside of his lip. 'Nice weather. Quite a change from Delhi.'

'Yes, the air's so fresh. And it's cold too.' She pulled her arms through the cardigan sleeves.

The old woman, who had earlier handed them the room keys, came with the lunch tray.

'How old is this place?' Abhay had asked her, fingering the heavy brass key as he waited for the porter to bring the luggage from the taxi. Megha wandered around the parlour to stand in front of the black-and-white picture of an English couple who posed with tennis racquets. 'Over seventy years,' the old woman replied. She and her husband had bought it some forty years ago from the English couple, and since then they had been welcoming guests summer and winter.

She set down the tray. Her coarse checked pants matched the blankets in the room. 'Let me know if you need anything,' she said and left.

Megha had ordered pasta and Abhay a chicken burger, the only two things that were on the menu that afternoon.

'I'm thinking of taking a walk later,' Abhay said. 'You can join me if you like.'

'I'm a bit tired. I'll freshen up and catch up with you in the evening.'

'Sure.'

'Have you read Ruskin Bond?' she said, wrapping the spaghetti around her fork.

'Don't think so.'

'You must have read him in school. Anyway, he lives here in Landour. I plan to go see his house.'

'I think I've seen him in the papers. Is his house on the tourist map?'

'I hope not.' She laughed.

She didn't laugh much, he realized. On the train, they had sat quietly, she behind a magazine and he poring over the morning papers. When they got off the train at Dehradun, she walked ahead of him in her slow, deliberate way. Though you don't have much of an ass to swing, he thought and laughed in his head.

Megha looked up from the pasta. 'Why are you smirking?'

'Nothing.' He waved it off. 'I just remembered something.'

A mynah swooped down from a nearby tree. It circled the lawn on its skinny, yellow legs. Abhay threw it a piece of bread. The bird looked at the morsel suspiciously and flew to sit on the sloping roof of the cottage.

Back in the room, Abhay opened his bag and put on a green hoodie. On the way out, he stopped in the bathroom to run a hairbrush through his hair, which was beginning to grey prematurely at twenty-nine. After his mother and some friends urged him, he had started to colour it. And then he met Kavya. That evening he hadn't touched up the greys in his sideburns and at the temples. She told him later that she thought the grey hair added to his sex appeal. He laughed. 'Nobody's ever said that,' he said. He stopped colouring it soon after. He took out the Blackberry from his pocket and checked the messages. Still nothing from her. 'Good,' he said.

Outside the cottage, the road sloped on one side and rose on the other. He turned to go uphill, for the extra exercise. His stomach was beginning to shape like a mound. He went to the gym every other evening now, but the Chivas later in the night didn't help. Kavya always knew if he was drinking while on the phone with her. 'Are you drinking?' she would ask. 'How the hell do you know?' 'I could hear you unscrew the cap.' 'On the phone? How?' She was sharp. Sometimes she made him uncomfortable.

A mule driver was leading his pack down the road. The hoofs made clucking sounds. Abhay walked on, hands deep in his pockets. The mountainside, terraced to make roads, was overgrown with moss.

He had come to Mussoorie regularly as a child. His father loved the hill station so much that they never went anywhere else for holidays. Sometimes as a compromise, they would stop en route at Haridwar and Rishikesh. At thirteen, when he refused to spend another vacation in Mussoorie, the family went without him. Next year he spent the summer in Calcutta where an uncle lived. The year after that, he visited cousins in Bombay. His relationship with his father had grown awkward with time, he had told Kavya one evening as he followed her around a store, looking at the china, candles and champagne glasses displayed like art. 'I'd sensed that,' she replied, running her fingers over the rim of a plate with a floral motif. She had luminous skin and straight, shoulder-length hair that she would sometimes pile in an unflattering topknot. 'You only talk about the buildings he's designed, the awards he's won, the politicians he knows,' she said, 'but never mention small things, bits of conversation you might have had with him.' Abhay rapped a whisky glass with a fingernail and nodded. Kavya selected red candles. 'What do you need three for?' he asked as he gave the cashier his credit card. 'I like to light them at night.' 'Do you light them when you talk with me?' 'Sometimes,' she shrugged. He shook his head. As they stepped out of the shop, she said, 'So tell me, on a scale of one to five, how would you rate your rapport with your father?' 'Zero,' he replied, and they burst out laughing.

He reached the marketplace, which the cottage owner had said was the Sisters Bazaar. 'Did a pair of sisters live there once? Or nuns?' he had asked after a second's thought. She told him it was named after the nurses who used to live there and work at the British hospital, tending soldiers during colonial times. The bazaar was five shops in all, made of heavy wood and packed together in a neat row. It looked quiet and old, something that would fit better with nuns counting beads on a rosary rather than with nurses scrambling from ward to ward. Landour reminded him of villages in Switzerland, serene and picturesque – so different from Mussoorie with its crowded Mall Road, choked with the smell of exhaust from taxis, horseshit everywhere.

He went into one of the shops. On the rack were canned food, cheese and freshly baked bread. There was a whole wall of books on India, with a shelf dedicated to Ruskin Bond. Abhay bought a copy of Bond's *Landour Days: A Writer's Journal.*

It was drizzling when he came out. The road was wet and the air smelled of tree bark and leaves. He tucked the book in the back of his jeans, zipped up the hoodie and turned towards the cottage. The mountain air invigorated him. He hummed as he walked.

Close to the cottage, he came upon a row of teashops with benches outside, and a guesthouse above, where two foreigners sat in a window smoking, a man in a kurta and a girl in a pink kameez. Abhay entered a teashop.

He looked through the menu on the chalkboard, asked for a ginger tea and lit a cigarette.

'Pretty fancy,' he said to the shopkeeper, waving the cigarette at the chalkboard. Besides ginger tea, there were waffles, pancakes and cheese sandwiches.

'Lots of foreigners come here, sir. That's why.'

'Yes, saw two in the window upstairs,' Abhay said. He went to sit at the single table in the corner.

'They come here to learn Hindi. They stay for months at times.' The shopkeeper added ginger and sugar to the water on the stove.

'So what all's there to see in Landour?'

'It's a small cantonment, sir. There's a church a few steps from here, St Paul's. But it would be closed at this hour. Then there's Lal Tibba from where you can see the Himalayas through a telescope set at the edge of the valley.'

He brought the tea to the table.

'Do you own the guest rooms upstairs?'

'Yes, sir.'

Abhay sipped the tea. It was sweet and strong. His father would have liked this industrious man, in his baggy trousers and checked sweater, making the best of his opportunities. In the days of his apprenticeship, his father used to cycle to construction sites, sometimes more than ten kilometres there and back. Now he was one of the top architects in Delhi. He still rose at four every morning, made a cup of tea, and worked in his study until eight before starting the day at the office. He earned from one project what Abhay made in a year. Several young architects who had joined his father's firm were now more successful than Abhay. Many had launched their own practice and one had gone on to design buildings in New York. His father would be disappointed that he was spending the weekend in Landour instead of working on his projects. But electrical and plumbing plans bored him, cost analyses and presentations bored him. In fact, constructing structures that rooted one down was the opposite of what he really wanted to do – wander, drift, lose himself on some long, meandering road. He lit another cigarette, drank the last of the tea and said goodbye to the shopkeeper. Daylight was receding as he walked back to the cottage, and darkness crept over the valley. The tip of his cigarette glowed brightly in the cold air.

A log fire was burning in the dining room. The orange light of the flames flickered over the stone wall. Abhay wondered if Megha was out or still in her room. He settled into a carrot-coloured sofa and asked the porter, who doubled as a waiter, for a whisky. A middle-aged couple sat by the window. He looked through *Landour Days*, but the light was not conducive to reading and he put it aside.

'When did you get back?' Megha walked in, a folder clutched under one arm.

'Just now. It was great. You should have come.'

'I did go out actually.' She sat down opposite him. 'It started to rain and it smelled so nice that I couldn't stay in my room any longer.'

The porter brought the whisky. Megha asked for a rum and Coke. Abhay showed her *Landour Days*.

'I haven't read this one,' she said, scanning the back cover.

'You can borrow it if you want.'

'Thanks, but I have this to keep myself busy.' She unclasped the folder and took out a sheaf of papers. 'I need to edit this piece for the coming issue. It's so badly written.' The porter brought the rum and Coke. She took a big sip, sat back, and started to mark the piece with a red pen.

The man by the window said something and the woman laughed. She tore a chapati in half and put it on his plate.

'How long have you been working?' Abhay asked.

'On this?'

'No, generally.'

She shut one eye as she calculated. 'Eight years. Five in Bombay ... nearly three in Delhi.'

Abhay sipped from his glass, and Megha returned to the piece. He looked at his phone. There was still no message from Kavya. 'Good,' he said to himself.

Abhay and Kavya had met on a February evening. A mutual friend had set the date. The two sat on the terrace at Café Turtle, drinking coffee and talking about travel and growing up in Delhi. They discussed the general elections and the new prime minister Manmohan Singh, cricket and their love for Sachin Tendulkar. But there was 'no spark' as Kavya later said to him. One night on the phone, she told him that when she first saw him, she thought he seemed like someone who was incapable of love. Abhay put the remote to one side. The TV was on mute. 'It might be true,' he said. 'But why did you think that?' She was good at this, this psychoanalysis. And he found it interesting to see himself from the outside. 'It's hard to say. You just seemed detached from everything. Okay, your turn now. What did you think of me?' He imagined her sitting up and crossing her legs, candles lit around the room. 'Intelligent. Engaging.' 'Not pretty?' 'Pretty too.' He laughed.

Kavya invited him over to do a past life regression with her. She did tarot readings as well. There were three cars in the long driveway, the last one a sleek model fitted with a grey cover. He met her mother having tea in the living room and getting her feet massaged by a maid. Kavya took him to the drawing room. She closed the sliding doors. 'Lie down.' She pointed to the couch. He laughed but did as she said. She sat down in a chair and told him to close his eyes. Slowly, she guided him through the relaxation process. 'Tell me what you see.' 'I can still feel everything. I'm still me,' he said, eyes fluttering. 'Of course you are. I haven't put you under a spell!' They started again. Abhay saw himself as a gypsy in Europe, who travelled in the countryside and through small towns with his caravan. He fell in love with a country girl, and for ten days they met every evening at the local fair. At night they sat around the campfire while the gypsies drank and sang songs. He said goodbye to her when the caravan was ready to move. Abhay felt like he was repeating a scene from a movie, but he could sense Kavya hanging on to every word. 'Did you get married in this life?' she asked. He shook his head. Kavya brought him back to the present. She raised his chin with her fingers. 'Now we know why you like to travel so much.' Her eyes twinkled. Abhay kissed her. Their lips felt dry against each other's, and he put his arm around her waist and drew her closer. The maid knocked at the door. Kavya nudged Abhay away and sat back in the chair. The maid brought in glasses of freshly squeezed orange juice and set them on the table. For a week after that, Abhay did not take her calls. He texted later to apologize for the kiss and for not calling her back. She told him it was okay.

Abhay and Megha finished dinner and went out for a stroll. The road lay in shadows with only a stretch, now and then, washed in street light. Abhay lit a cigarette. Megha took one too.

'I didn't know you smoked,' he said.

'Not really. I'm always trying to quit.' She exhaled through the side of her mouth.

It was only eight thirty, but the town seemed asleep. The two took deep puffs on their cigarettes, their footsteps making scraping sounds.

Megha told him about an art exhibition she had recently attended, then talked about her job, the workload, the long hours. She stubbed the cigarette on the mountainside, charring some moss with it. He liked that she was independent, lived in Delhi away from her parents who were in Lucknow, and earned her own living.

They sat by the roadside and watched the lights on the mountain opposite.

'Want to have another drink?' she asked.

'I've got some Chivas. We could drink it in my room. They would have closed the dining room by now.'

'Sure. Why not.'

Abhay got ice from downstairs. Megha brought a glass from her room. He poured them a drink each, while she sat on the bed, riffling through the music on his iPod. She put on Nat King Cole. *'Blue moon...'* he sang. Abhay drew the chair close to the bed and settled down with his glass. Megha swung her foot lightly to the music. It was strange how she never asked anything about him, he thought. She was so wrapped up in herself. That was Kavya's phrase. She used it often for him.

Megha fixed them another drink. She gave Abhay his glass and came and sat back on the bed. *'The falling leaves drift by the window,'* Nat King Cole was singing, *'the autumn leaves of red and gold.'* She swirled the Chivas, making the ice clink. Abhay wanted to kiss the cool tips of her fingers, to taste the whisky on her breath. Megha lifted one foot and set it on his knee. He caressed her between the toes and they continued to sip at the whisky. He moved to the bed and they slipped out of their clothes. The light from the lamps made the room honey coloured. Megha slept naked that night under the worn white sheets and the checked blanket, and he in a pair of boxers and T-shirt.

After she returned to her room in the morning, Abhay got up and parted the curtains. Sunlight streamed in. Across the valley a red car laboured up the mountain road, hiding in and emerging from the foliage. He checked his phone. There was a call from his mother. He smoked a cigarette and called her back.

Kavya had phoned him late one night. 'Can you pick me up?' She sounded drunk. 'From where?' He squinted at the clock on the bedside table. 'It's the middle of the night.'

'It's not the middle of the night. It's two o'clock, if you must know,' she said, slurring every other word. 'I came to a friend's wedding and now I can't find my driver.' Abhay groaned. 'What's the address?'

He found her standing at the entrance of the marquee in a lime-green sari that glittered with Swarovski crystals, sandals in one hand. Abhay helped her into the car.

'My feet are blistered from all the dancing.' She turned on the car light and checked her toes. 'You shouldn't have danced so much then.' He flicked off the light and turned the key in the ignition. 'You look pretty, by the way.' She put her head back and shut her eyes. He thought she had dozed off, but then she said, 'Why can't we be in a relationship, Abhay?' He chewed on the inside of his lip and concentrated on the road. 'Why?' she asked again. 'Because I don't want to be in one.' Because sooner rather than later you would want to talk about the future, he thought. She stayed quiet. 'I like how we are,' he said. 'We talk almost every day. We meet now and then. I don't want to say it, but it is like a relationship.' He pulled over outside her house. 'We should stop talking so much then,' she said as she left the car.

He caved in after a few days. 'Let's give it a try,' he called to say. 'If you insist.' She laughed. Nothing much changed between them. They talked like they did before, about the same things, in the same tone, and that made Abhay relax. He even felt happy about the relationship. Then Kavya asked him to meet her, asked him three times in the same day, and he lost his cool. 'I don't like being pushed. Stop pushing me.' They broke up and resumed their friendship.

He showered and went downstairs for breakfast. Megha was there already, eating fried egg and sipping juice. She looked up when he walked in.

'Nice day,' she said, pointing to the clear light that slanted in through the window.

Abhay smiled. 'A cheese omelette and tea,' he said to the porter.

'Yes, sir.' He bowed and went to the kitchen.

'I was thinking of going to Lal Tibba. Would you like to come along?' Megha said

Abhay chewed on the inside of his lip. He glanced at the couple from last night having tea two tables away.

'You don't have to.' Megha's knife and fork made clinking sounds on the plate. 'I just thought I'd check with you.'

'No, I'll join you. It's okay.' The light from the window lay trapped on the floor in a rectangle.

Megha plucked a wild, white flower from the roadside and twirled it as they walked. The day was pleasant. Birds chirped in the valley.

'Do you know you can see the Himalayas from Lal Tibba?' she said. Her mole glistened in the daylight.

He nodded.

'I'm writing a travel essay on Landour.'

'You are? That's nice.'

Two women passed by carrying firewood on their heads and talking in the hillside dialect. Both wore flower-shaped nose pins.

'I wanted to start a travel business,' Abhay told her. 'Not the usual kind, but something bespoke that might interest an elite, rich traveller. I was planning custom-made itineraries for Europe. You know, castles in Ireland, chalets in France.'

'Why didn't you then?' She looked at him.

'I couldn't get a business model together.' His father had refused to give him a loan, said it wasn't a viable venture. There were already too many operators, he had added, sitting in his high-back leather chair. Abhay tried for months to get a loan from a bank and to work it out on his own. He and Kavya spent hours composing travel itineraries.

The climb got steep. The valley was thick with deodars and so were the mountains. Here and there were some private cottages.

At Lal Tibba, Abhay paid for the tickets and they took turns looking through the eyepiece of the telescope. The Himalayas didn't look as majestic as they had expected, just regular snow-capped peaks in the distance.

'That was a bit lame,' Megha said as they started back.

'Yeah, a waste of a morning.'

They stopped at the teashop for lunch and ordered coffee and sandwiches, which they ate sitting on the benches outside. A foreigner joined them with her tea. She had ginger hair and freckled arms.

'Are you studying at the school?' Abhay asked.

'Yes, I'm learning Sanskrit.'

'And where are you from?'

'Germany.'

Megha turned to the shopkeeper. 'Would you know where Ruskin Bond's house is?'

'It's just down the road, madam.' He put his head out of the shop and pointed to the right. 'It's the house with green shutters on the windows.'

'You want to come along?' she asked Abhay.

'Not really.' He shrugged.

'I think I should go see it for my essay.' She finished the coffee and put the mug to one side. 'I'll meet you at the cottage then.' She touched Abhay on the shoulder and walked off in her slow, deliberate way.

Abhay lit a cigarette. 'Why do you want to learn Sanskrit?'

'I want to read the Mahabharata, the Gita especially. I've wanted to do that ever since I saw the TV show some years ago.'

He laughed. 'I don't know many Indians, not young ones at least, who have read it. We just watch it on TV.'

This time the girl laughed.

Abhay paid for the coffee and sandwiches and started towards the cottage. The sun was behind clouds. Mist had rolled down from the valley on to the road, obscuring it in parts. When he walked through a patch of mist, it left cool drops on his face.

At the cottage he sat on the lawn, under the wide umbrella, even though it was cloudy. A mynah hopped around the grass. He wondered if it was the same one as yesterday. Its eyes were as yellow as its legs. Abhay wished he was staying another day or two. He wondered if he should tell Megha to catch the train by herself tomorrow. She should be okay with it. Kavya would have grumbled. He checked his phone. There was still no message from her. He took a picture of the bird and of the valley.

The last time he met Kavya, it was in the evening at a café in Khan market. He had come straight from a construction site and was famished. She spent fifteen minutes deliberating over the menu. Finally, she decided on a cheesecake. He asked for an onion soup and a sandwich. 'Can you bring it quickly?' he said to the waiter.

He sat back in the chair and shook his foot. 'Why don't you do something with your life?' he said to her. 'Why? I'm doing what I enjoy.' She was going on a week-long meditation camp to Dharamshala. 'Which is what? Sitting around and wasting your time?' Her forehead creased. 'Don't take that tone with me, Abhay.' 'No, you are so full of ideas about how I should get my life together, why don't you apply some to yourself,' he said. She looked away and watched the orange walls of the café. 'Why don't you marry one of the guys your parents keep introducing you to?' She was looking over his shoulder. Abhay turned around. It was a poster of a French bathtub. 'You are pretty fucked up, if you ask me,' he said.

She flushed, eyes still on the poster. She got up and left. He messaged her the next day to apologize, but she hadn't replied in two weeks.

When Megha came back, he was still sitting on the lawn. She suggested they go down to Mussoorie for a bit.

The Mall Road was thick with honeymooning couples and children taking horse rides. Abhay bought a corncob from an old man who squatted by the roadside with his coal grill. Megha stepped into dusty shops to try on artificial jewellery. Abhay hung in the background, munching corn. She bought a pair of large, tear-shaped earrings with filigree work. He thought them ugly, but when she asked him, he said they were fine. They roamed around the stalls of Tibetan refugees, where women in long black skirts and faces lined with wrinkles sold accessories and oddities. When Abhay was eight, his father had bought him a compass from one of these stalls. It had a bronze cover and was as thin as a pocket mirror. He looked for a similar compass among the wares. Heavy drops of rain started to fall. The women covered the stalls with blue tarpaulin.

Abhay and Megha returned to the cottage. They drank in the dining room, had dinner and went out for a walk, came back and drank some more, this time in Megha's room, and slept together. In the morning Abhay went back to his room.

'Do you have any plans before we leave?' he said over breakfast.

She took some butter and spread it on her toast. 'I want to start working on the essay.'

'All right, so I'll meet you in the parlour at one.'

Abhay went out by himself. The church was open. It was small and quiet, exposed wooden beams in the ceiling, pale yellow walls. He sat there for some time and then walked to the Sisters Bazaar. On the way back, he noticed the house with green window shutters.

Abhay and Megha waited in the parlour with their bags. The old owner sat at the desk, leafing through a magazine. He checked his Blackberry. Still nothing.

The taxi arrived, and the porter carried the bags outside and deposited them in the dicky.

Abhay gave him a hundred-rupee note. 'Do you have any children?'

The porter nodded.

He took out another hundred and stuffed it into the porter's pocket.

The porter smiled. Deep creases showed on his face. 'Come back next year,' he said as Abhay and Megha got into the car.

KETTLE ON THE HOB

Inside a Chekhov Play

The kettle is made of aluminium, a wood bail handle. It's old, it's moody. It takes half an hour to get the water barely hot enough. Kavya likes to start her mornings with chai, David sips hibiscus or mint tea all day long as he paints, and the evening tea together on the balcony may soon become a ritual, which means the kettle stays on the hob pretty much the whole day. 'It's as though we're inside a Chekhov play,' David likes to say, 'where the samovar is kept going at all hours.' The kettle is, in fact, on the hob right now, while Kavya waits at the dining table in her striped pajama and yellow T-shirt and David rinses his brushes and sets them in a row to dry. He taps the kettle to check if it is warming up, orange paint under his fingernails, a couple of spots on the wrist. He pours the water over the Taj Mahal teabags that Kavya has brought along all the way from India and whose bold flavour he has come to enjoy. He passes her a cup, and they move to the balcony where the metal chairs are still warm from the sun. 'At the class today,' she tells him, 'we had to close our eyes and quiet our minds until some physical feature of a loved one emerged. I saw my grandmother's hands: small, square, patterned with age spots. I was surprised at how clearly I remembered them. I was surprised because I had never thought of her as someone I loved ... It took me back to some happy times in my childhood.' 'That's nice,' David says. 'Let me try it too.' He crosses his ankles, shuts his eyes. He sees five-year-old Theo fixing stumps in the backyard. Such innocence, such focus, soft blonde hair, ears that stick out. David tries to see a semblance of himself in his son; he always thinks Theo's nose is at least a little bit crooked, like his own. 'I miss him,' he sighs, 'but if I were home there would be no time to paint.' David and Kavya exchange a smile. They sip at their tea. 'You think it's possible the exercise is meant to unlock emotions and memories?' she says. David shrugs. Kavya shrugs, for she isn't sure either. Below, Rue Saint-Jacques is stretched in shade, with only the Val-de-Grâce on the far side washed in sunlight, its ancient dome a tarnished green. In the apartment across the road, the white-haired woman with bony shoulders – who they've decided is Turkish – surveys the road and sips her coffee carefully so as not to burn her mouth, making Kavya and David wish their tea was at least a little bit hot. They console themselves with the idea of being inside a play.

Parisian Nights

There is no air conditioning, not even a ceiling fan. As if to tease, there hangs opposite the bed a charcoal drawing of a tree on a breezy day. Kavya's limbs feel sticky, the pillow warm. She's upset with David for claiming the room that looks on to the street and leaving her the windowless one across from the bathroom, when she's paid full rent and he's here on the patronage of the landlord. She fluffs the pillow and turns it over. She briefly considers a classmate's suggestion of sleeping naked. She fans herself with a hand fan that she found in the bedside drawer. She gets up and plods out. In the moonlight the living room appears less dingy, the crochet curtains in the French windows are delicate, the kettle manages a faint glint, it is hard to tell the carpet is worn. Her parents don't know she shares the apartment with a man. She picked it because the classes are held right across the road, in an old building next to the Schola Cantorum. She opens a window and steps out. It is warm, but there is a breeze. The Turkish woman is still watching TV. The homeless man sleeps on the pavement, a shabby bundle. Kavya settles in the metal chair. She breathes in the calm night and breathes out her frustration. Deep breath in, breath out. Love in, anger out. From the street comes laughter, hushed chatter in French. She peers over the railing as a bunch of youngsters stumble out of the jazz bar, its neon sign lit red. One of them starts to sing, a billowing opera-like song, and the others join in. Could be students from the Schola Cantorum. There is an abandon about their unsteady gait, their swaying arms, their full voices, a freedom Kavya wishes for herself. She pulls up her knees, tucks them under her chin. She passed the last five years in virtual house arrest. She read in her room, meditated, cleansed her chakras, paced the driveway in the evenings until the cars returned home. She went to bed early, woke up late. The window in her room looked on to the back wall of the adjacent house. The group moves down the street and the song grows faint. She returns indoors and lies down on the couch. Parisian apartments ought to have fans.

Honey

Late afternoon, sun mellow; David painting a red and brown zigzag pattern; Kavya penning a journal entry; the kettle refusing to warm up. David looks from the side of the canvas. 'Honey, why are you home all the time?' His question takes Kavya by surprise. She blinks. 'Umm ... I haven't made any friends yet. It's a new city ... Alone, I feel I might get lost.' Every day after class, she returns to the apartment, eats lunch – leftovers or a baguette she has picked from the little plaza opposite the Val-de-Grâce – writes in her journal, takes very long baths, meditates in her room. After tea David goes out for a stroll or will meet up with a friend, and when he returns she's still there in her striped pajama and yellow T-shirt, curled up on the couch with *The Art of Happiness*, or stirring one of the precooked curries she has brought from home. They talk, he'll try some curry, show her pictures he's taken to send to Theo: a miniature carousel in a shop window, a fierce gargoyle, a tiny car parked in a street. 'Honey, you are young,' he says now, 'and this is Paris. You must go out. Don't wait around for people to accompany you.' She nods. She turned thirty this year. She doesn't feel young any more, but she likes him saying it. There's a certain homeliness about David that makes him easy to relate to; her classmates, ironically, she finds quite worldly. They attend retreats and conferences; one has trekked to the top of the Kilimanjaro; another, a Hollywood writer, wears chic ethnic clothes and excellent make-up. They talk about their love affairs, their travels, meeting the Dalai Lama, or bounce off lines from *Star Trek*, to all of which she has nothing to contribute. It makes her feel as though she has resurfaced into society after years and years of being submerged. At home she went out once a week, for lunch, or to buy books, sometimes to shop for clothes, and her mother made sure to chaperone her. Tomorrow afternoon, however, David is going to give her a map and push her out of the apartment.

Green Dots

Most mornings Kavya wakes up to find David at the easel, one arm behind his back, patiently painting green dot after green dot, some light, some dark, some translucent, some dense. When she looks in from the kitchen, the green molecules seem to shift, like the wind, like a placid sea. This will be David's first solo show in ten years, and he's pleased it is with an 'important London gallery'. He lives in Sheffield, where his wife is a lawyer, and he stays at home to look after Theo. He paints in the mornings while the house is still sleeping and rain falls outside the attic window. For some reason, Kavya has come to think of Sheffield as a town of frequent rains and thunderstorms. She imagines David and Theo making paper boats all day long and setting them sail in rivulets outside the house. Over a Saturday breakfast of toast, tomatoes and cheese, she learns that he used to paint self-portraits in oil, but following Theo's birth transitioned to spontaneous patterns of lines, grids and dots. The kettle is being stubborn, and David is at the hob tweaking the regulator. 'Theo's brought playfulness to my life. I mean, it's just marvellous sometimes to watch him build a tower of Legos, then knock it down and instantly start building again.' Piano notes waft in through the French windows, the morning class at the Schola Cantorum reaching its zenith. 'More and more, it makes me wonder if everything is just play, our jobs, the things we do, my art.' He looks over his shoulder at Kavya and adds, 'Maybe even all of life, all existence.' 'Do you know about Leela?' she asks. He thinks, then shakes his head. 'Leela is the concept of divine play.' She joins him at the hob. She taps the kettle. 'It holds that God created the world just for the joy of creation. God created it out of bliss, for bliss.' She moves the kettle to a different hotplate, for sometimes that helps. David turns on the regulator. 'This perverse kettle, however, is the very opposite of bliss,' she quips. David laughs. His silver chain, his crooked nose, his paint marked T-shirt. Kavya feels a longing, though not for him alone, but his life, his work, his love for his son, and how it all fulfils him. The green dots multiply over the next week to cover the huge canvas.

Straight Lines, Right Angles

Often Kavya will amble along Rue Saint-Jacques, past the glimpse of the Pantheon's white columns, the uphill stretch to the Sorbonne, the intersection of St Germain, the lively alleys of bistros and bars, until she reaches the Seine with the Notre-Dame and its magnificent cobweb-like windows rising above the bank, and then she will trace her steps back to the apartment. Lately she has discovered that a left turn down a cobbled alley close to the apartment leads to the Luxembourg Gardens. Here she sits some afternoons, describing in her journal the kids skipping around the pond in sandals nudging their sailboats with sticks, the African nanny feeding a chubby baby, a lone cloud on the terribly blue sky, the man with beautiful lips snoozing behind his Ray-Bans, an old couple in sunhats. The programme encourages maintaining an account of their time in the city. *All Journeys Lead Inwards* has invited participants to spend four weeks in Paris, soak in the city, and reflect on the self. The idea is to place yourself through displacement; that living in a new environment, an unfamiliar setup, can offer a glimpse into our real selves. The programme is run by a French traveller who converted to Buddhism. The classes take place in a hundred-year-old sun-filled room with cornice mouldings and a chequered floor, where the students sit cross-legged on cushions placed along the walls. When the instructor takes the class on a tour of the Louvre, Kavya finds out that a left turn at the Seine and some more walking under the Parisian sun gets one to the heart of the city. David encourages her to take the metro to the other side to visit the Sacré-Cœur, but this she plainly refuses on account of being unable to read the signs. She's determined to explore the city in straight lines and at right angles.

The Sad Demise

She smells fumes as she enters the apartment. Coughing, swatting at the air, she rushes in. She finds the kettle on the hob, quivering, smoky, the hotplate a howling red, and David painting peacefully, *Gymnopédie No. 1* playing on his laptop, smoke swirling over his head. 'Oh my God, David, you're going to burn down the place!' In one quick movement she lifts the kettle, turns on the faucet and ducks it under the stream. David peers over the top of the canvas. The kettle sizzles, issuing thick smoke. The kettle was an old soul, perhaps on its last cycle of birth and rebirth. Yet it tirelessly offered tepid tea, one cup after another. It kept David company through the day as he worked alone. Its tardiness added charm to life in this dingy apartment. Tealess that evening, they mourn its passing. They drink David's red wine, so cheap it tastes like poison. They muse over the possibility of Kavya falling in love with a Frenchman, settling down in Paris and buying this apartment where the kettle saw its last days. David, who'll always talk about his son but seldom about his wife, turns out to be a romantic. Kavya nibbles at crackers in order to keep down the wine. David confesses he was surprised when he learned she didn't have a boyfriend. There was something about the way she carried herself, holding away from everything, that suggested a relationship ... 'Or perhaps it was the ghost of one,' he adds, looking sideways at her, holding her gaze. 'The relationship ended many years ago. Because my parents didn't approve.' 'Oh. Oh honey.' He reaches for her hand. She has never talked about this with anyone, but now she has an impulse to tell David about the solitary years, the confinement, her cold relationship with her parents, the humiliating way her mother kept an eye on her, the fading away of her youth, the passage of half a decade.

She wants to say all this out loud. She would like someone to hear her story, and then perhaps she can leave it behind in Paris, on this balcony on Rue Saint-Jacques. But she waits too long. The moment passes. David refills their glasses and raises a toast to the kettle. They drink the wretched wine. The homeless man paces back and forth, mumbling to himself. Somewhere behind them, the Eiffel Tower lights up.

The Lock

It's a small but packed crêperie in Montparnasse. David's ordered a chicken mushroom crêpe, and his friend Laura a chocolate one and red wine. David tells her that Theo rode his bike without training wheels for the first time today, and he's disappointed to have missed it. Laura has a nasal laugh, a complexion that gets ruddier with wine. She thinks parenthood a great distraction, children a luxury. She's followed her subject for nearly two decades and painted an object the subject has felt attached to each year from adolescence into manhood. She has plans for her and David to attend a couple of gallery openings later in the evening. It's close to ten when David returns to the apartment. There's no light showing under the door, and he surmises that Kavya, who was out on a day trip to Versailles and Giverny with an American couple from her programme, has gone to bed. But as he's fishing the keys out of his pocket, there's a muffled but frantic banging deep inside the apartment. What was that? He touches his ear to the door. He knocks softly. Again the frantic pounding, a panicked voice, incomprehensible but possibly Kavya's. Could someone be holding her hostage inside? He considers running away, staying the night at Laura's. But what if it *is* Kavya? He chews at the collar of his shirt. He imagines himself dying without seeing Theo again. He imagines Theo growing up without him and forgetting him. He inhales and inserts the key in the lock. The apartment is dark but for the moonlight. Again the pounding, and Kavya's unmistakable voice issuing from the bathroom. He answers by calling her name. The handle on the bathroom door is jammed. She's been trapped in there for four hours, she says, ever since she returned from the excursion. He wrestles with the handle. He desperately pushes at the door with his shoulder. The lock's mechanism somehow falls into place. The door opens and Kavya bursts out. She's shaken, though she tries to smile. When she leans against David's chest, her petite frame is stiff, like Theo's after a nightmare.

Ding

They hate the new electric kettle. They resent it every time it gives them a piping hot cup of tea. *Ding* it goes in under 90 seconds, water mumbling and gurgling. They dislike it for its efficiency. They miss their darling old kettle. They miss fussing over it, cajoling it and cursing it. They miss lingering in the kitchen. They miss the sweet anticipation of tea. Now teatime is over too quickly, the cups rinsed and placed back until next time. They can no longer say to each other that they live inside a Chekhov play. They miss the comforting feeling of being inside a story, knowing their lives are being written out with thought and care.

Table for Two

Flâneuring along Boulevard St Michel, she eyes tarts and pastries in patisserie windows, she browses books on tables set on the pavement, she steps into a boutique and tries on a summer dress, she blesses her grandmother who in a way made all this possible for her. In her grandmother's last days, Kavya began visiting her alone at the hospital since her mother was busy with relatives and well-wishers at home. She would briefly sit by the bedside holding her grandmother's hand and then roam the hospital's corridors untethered, up and down the stairs, to the X-ray room, the ultrasound department, buy chocolate at the pharmacy, sit with tea and a muffin in the cafeteria. Her grandmother passed away, and her parents were so distracted worrying over the fate of the joint business and assets that when she asked if she could go to Paris they nodded. And here she is now, stopping for crème brûlée at a plaza with fountains and leafy trees. 'Salut, monsieur,' she greets the waiter. She picks a table for two outdoors. 'Une crème brûlée, s'il vous plaît?' She uses the little French she has picked up at the language class of the programme. 'Oui, madam,' the waiter says, pleased by her effort. It's a lazy Sunday, people sit around the fountains, pigeons tiptoe on the cobblestones, at the end of the plaza is an old building that looks like a church but probably isn't. 'Bon appétit.' The waiter sets down the dessert. The first bite melts in her mouth. She scoops a couple more. She notices how the other chair at her table is set against a tree so that it cannot be pulled out, making it essentially a table for one. No one can join her, even if he wanted to. She wonders if she is subconsciously keeping love from coming into her life. She is reminded of the ghost David mentioned. At the class tomorrow, when it's her turn to share her flâneuring experience, she will not speak about her realization and only describe the pleasure of having crème brûlée for the first time.

Leela

The art gallery has asked David to compose a text to accompany his upcoming exhibition *Leela*. He sits three mornings at the dining table sipping hibiscus tea and clicking his teeth with a pencil. In the end he has this:

> *The driveway is gravelled. Weeds have broken from between the pebbles. We play cricket and then croquet. Now the boy decides for us to tug and pull at the weeds*

and throw them in the bin. Back and forth, back and forth, back and forth. My knees ache. He thinks up a new game of hiding treasure under the gravel. So we gather what we can, a dry leaf, a yellow flower from the garden, a rotten strawberry, a twig, some gum and lint from my pocket, and bury it under the gravel. With his finger he marks the spot with a large X. We go inside. We eat dinner. It grows dark. The trees look nearly purple. We come out with a pocket torch to look for our treasure.

A Soirée

The apartment is transformed by the hubbub of guests, potted cacti, a stained-glass lamp on the paints table. The darling dead kettle is posing on the hob. Laura has helped with the arrangements and now stands by David's elbow as he shows his paintings to some friends. *Green Dots* is centre stage on the easel. Kavya is chatting with Bad-breath Jerome, who studies economics at the Sorbonne and paints in his free hours. Leaning away, holding the wine glass on her knee, she tells him about her programme, and he asks if she has indeed managed to 'place herself'. She doesn't talk about the table for two. Instead, she recounts her moment at the Church of St Séverin earlier this week, when she had an intense experience of being present. In that brief time, the past and the future fell away from her, leaving her sitting in the pew unencumbered, almost weightless. She watched the stained-glass windows grow remarkably vivid, the air was redolent of old stones and wood, and the scrape of a little girl's shoes as she tugged at her father's arm was so clear that she felt she had never heard a truer sound. She is shy saying all this, but surprisingly Jerome nods as though he can appreciate her experience. Two girls with shimmering eyelids and gorgeous lashes plonk themselves on the floor by the coffee table. Kavya wishes she was wearing the dress she had bought today at Galeries Lafayette along with gifts for her parents and Raghu and his wife. The girls chatter with Kavya and Jerome about their evening at Moulin Rouge with their respective boyfriends. Kavya shares that, in her four weeks, she didn't find a chance to see the Moulin Rouge or watch the Eiffel Tower lit at night or take a boat tour of the Seine. For these, she must return to Paris one day. Hopefully with a boyfriend, she adds, and all three girls giggle. Kavya looks across the room and finds David looking at her. *What?* she mouths. He shakes his head. He is surprisingly sombre. He's been drinking all evening. The girls leave, and Jerome laces his fingers with Kavya's. He grew up on a farm, he tells her, and feels out of place in Paris. His breath, subdued by wine and olives, is no longer as whiffy, and at some point in the night they might even kiss. The idea, though appealing, makes Kavya nervous. She excuses herself to get a drink of water. She fills a glass at the sink. The kettle looks downcast. The char on its surface has become a flaky layer. She pulls the kettle into the sink and soaps and scrubs it patiently, the outside first, then the inside. She manages to get most of the char and soot off. On an impulse, she fills it with water and puts it on. She rinses her water glass. She can see David on the balcony alone. She touches the kettle and, to her delight, finds it warming up. She darts to the balcony and tells David about the kettle's resurrection. She expected him to be elated but he only nods. 'I have something for you,' he says. 'Remind me to give it to you before your flight.' 'But I didn't get you anything.' 'That's okay, honey.' The Turkish woman too has guests tonight, and everyone is in the living room, drinking and laughing, kids running around. On the pavement, the homeless man is eating a sandwich. 'Can I tell you something?' David says. She nods. 'I don't think Theo's really my son.' Kavya is unsure of what to make of this. 'Something about the time of his conception doesn't add up. He bears a striking resemblance to one of our family friends.' Kavya inches closer and he wraps an arm around her shoulder. Behind them, their apartment is glowing with people and their happiness.

ACKNOWLEDGEMENTS

THANK YOU TO MY FRIENDS Kaninika Mishra and Nic Bouskill, who always made time to read my work, and to Lucretia Grindle for her encouragement.

Thank you to Amit Chaudhuri for his workshops at UEA where I glimpsed the bigger picture of this book.

I am grateful to the Virginia Center for the Creative Arts and Sangam House for my time spent writing at Mt San Angelo and Nrityagram, respectively, and to the magazines, journals and competitions that afforded homes to my stories.

My heartfelt gratitude to HarperCollins India, my editor Rahul Soni and publisher Udayan Mitra for their faith in this collection and for supporting it in every way possible.

Thank you to my daughter Tara, who has filled my world with joy, and to my husband Manu for everything. Without his love this book would not have been possible.

ABOUT THE AUTHOR

Sonal Kohli grew up in Delhi and now lives in Washington, D.C. She has an MA in Creative Writing from the University of East Anglia, UK, and a BA in Economics from Shri Ram College of Commerce, Delhi University. Her stories have been shortlisted for the Bristol Short Story Prize and the Fish Short Story Prize, and her first book, *The House Next to the Factory*, was long-listed for the Tata Literature Live! First Book Award 2022.

30 Years *of*

HarperCollins *Publishers* India

At HarperCollins, we believe in telling the best stories and finding the widest possible readership for our books in every format possible. We started publishing 30 years ago; a great deal has changed since then, but what has remained constant is the passion with which our authors write their books, the love with which readers receive them, and the sheer joy and excitement that we as publishers feel in being a part of the publishing process.

Over the years, we've had the pleasure of publishing some of the finest writing from the subcontinent and around the world, and some of the biggest bestsellers in India's publishing history. Our books and authors have won a phenomenal range of awards, and we ourselves have been named Publisher of the Year the greatest number of times. But nothing has meant more to us than the fact that millions of people have read the books we published, and somewhere, a book of ours might have made a difference.

As we step into our fourth decade, we go back to that one word – a word which has been a driving force for us all these years.

Read.